About the Author

DENNIS MILLER is the host of the five-time Emmy Award–winning talk show *Dennis Miller Live* and a former color commentator on *Monday Night Football*. He lives in California with his wife and two sons.

BOOKS BY DENNIS MILLER

The Rants

Ranting Again

I Rant, Therefore I Am

An All-Out Blitz Against
Soul-Sucking Jobs,
Twisted Child Stars,
Holistic Loons
& People Who Eat Their Dogs!

DENNIS MILLER

THE RANT ZONE

Perennial
An Imprint of HarperCollinsPublishers

A hardcover edition of this book was published in 2001 by HarperCollins Publishers.

THE RANT ZONE. Copyright © 2001 by Dennis Miller. All rights reserved. Printed in the United States of America. No part of this book may be used or reproduced in any manner whatsoever without written permission except in the case of brief quotations embodied in critical articles and reviews. For information address HarperCollins Publishers Inc., 10 East 53rd Street, New York, NY 10022.

HarperCollins books may be purchased for educational, business, or sales promotional use. For information please write: Special Markets Department, HarperCollins Publishers Inc., 10 East 53rd Street, New York, NY 10022.

First Perennial edition published 2002.

Designed by Elliott Beard

Library of Congress Cataloging-in-Publication Data is available.

ISBN 0-06-050537-0

02 03 04 05 06 ❖/RRD 10 9 8 7 6 5 4 3 2 1

Acknowledgments

Much of the material in *The Rant Zone* originally appeared on my HBO show *Dennis Miller Live*. I'd like to thank Jose Arroyo, David Feldman, Eddie Feldman, Jim Hanna, Leah Krinsky, Kirsten McFarland, Jacob Weinstein, and David Weiss for their assistance. I'd also like to thank my extraordinarily patient and vigilant editor, David Hirshey. Also Rob Kurtner, Michele DeVoe, Colleen Grillo, Marc Gurvitz, Debbie Palacio, Matt Perl, Kevin Slattery, and I'd especially like to thank all my friends at HBO, with a special thanks to Jeff Bewkes, Chris Albrecht, Carolyn Strauss, and Sarah Condon, who makes it all possible. Now, I don't want to get off on a rant here, but . . .

Contents

Child Stars
MIKEY HATES IT!   1

'50s Television
A GOLDEN SHOWER OF PRAISE FOR TV   5

Women in Sports
JOCKS WITHOUT CUPS   9

Alt.Medicine
GINGKO, SHMINKO!   13

Lousy Jobs
MINIMUM WAGES OF SIN   17

Revenge
I JUST CALLED TO SAY "FUCK OFF"   21

God
HIGH AND MIGHTY PISSED   25

CONTENTS

Patriotism
    OF THEE I SNARL   29

The Penis
    SCHLONG'S DAY JOURNEY INTO NIGHT   31

Man's Dark Side
    SATAN'S LITTLE HELPERS   35

Education
    SCHOOLS FOR SCANDAL   39

Friendship
    PAL DENNY   43

Elvis
    MEMPHIS SLIM . . . OR FAT   45

Female President
    ANYTHING HE CAN DO, SHE CAN DO BETTER   49

Insurance Companies
    A PREMIUM SCREWING   53

Auto Shopping
    THAT NEW-CAR STENCH   57

Big Government
    TIME TO TIGHTEN THE BELTWAY   61

Travel
    ALL THE DISCOMFORTS OF HOME   65

The Sopranos
    MOB RULES   69

CONTENTS

Horror Movies
FREDDIE GETS THE FINGER
73

Rage
MAD AS HELL AND NOT GOING TO FAKE IT ANYMORE!
77

The English Language
ME TALK REAL GOOD
81

Show Business
HOLLYWOOD AND VAIN
85

Intolerance
TWELVE MILLION ANGRY MEN
89

Music Business
A SOUND DIVESTMENT
93

The Clintons
IS HE GONE YET?
97

Shrinks
PSYCHIATRIC COUCH POTATOES
101

Credit/Debt
BET YOU CAN'T BORROW JUST ONE
105

Hipsters
GOOD-BYE, COOL, COOL WORLD
109

Extreme Sports
DON'T TRY THIS AT HOME . . . WE REALLY MEAN IT THIS TIME
113

CONTENTS

Media/Privacy
UP NEXT: YOUR COLONOSCOPY ON *20/20*! 117

Buying Stocks
**TIPS FOR INVESTING
IN A BULLSHIT MARKET** 121

Reality Shows
SURVIVING *SURVIVOR* 125

Tobacco Industry
WHERE THERE'S SMOKE, THERE'S PROFIT 129

TV Ads
LIFE IS A PITCH 133

Crime and Punishment
HE GOT THE SOFA . . . AND THE CHAIR 137

Death
THE BIG SNOOZE 141

Civil Disobedience
TO THE BARRICADES . . . IN SUVs 145

The Energy Crisis
CALIFORNIA REAMIN' 149

Anxiety
**DON'T PANIC . . .
OOPS, YOU'RE RIGHT, PANIC** 153

Bureaucracy
LIVING AND DYING IN TRIPLICATE 157

Marriage
WEDDING DISS 161

Why Football Has Replaced Baseball as the National Pastime
"WELL, ISN'T IT OBVIOUS?" 165

The Super Bowl
"THE MAIN EVENT" 169

The XFL
WRESTLING WITH YOUR SUBCONSCIOUS 173

Fans
YOU'RE NO. 1! YOU'RE NO. 1! 179

Sports Talk
FIRST-TIME CALLER, LONG-TIME RANTER 183

Sex in D.C.
JUST THE TIP OF THE VICE-BERG 189

Remorse
EVERYBODY'S GUILTY . . . EXCEPT O.J. 193

Child Stars

MIKEY HATES IT!

If Mr. Blackwell has come out of his lover's hole and seen his shadow, it must be awards season, huh? I watched the People's Choice awards the other night, and I'm torn when I see that little kid from *The Sixth Sense*. On the one hand, you'd like to see him win, and on the other, for his own good, you wish he wasn't even in the business.

Now, I don't want to get off on a rant here, but I'm reasonably sure that acting isn't a suitable profession for adults, let alone children. These days, every movie ends with the assurance that "no animals were injured in the making of this film." Yeah, but they never tell you about the kids, do they?

Child actors are a tragedy waiting to happen. Look at the Little Rascals. They're all dead. Now, sure, they pretty much all died of old age, but does that make them any less dead? O-tay, then. Where was I? Oh, yeah, the harsh reality of a child star segueing into his or her most challenging role: adulthood. Life cereal is running a new series of commercials featuring a grown-up Mikey. Remember Mikey? The "Mikey-likes-it" Mikey? Well, get this: Life cereal cast some other guy to play the adult Mikey! Nice, huh? So where is the real Mikey? No doubt he's sitting in a dimly lit bar in the Valley midafternoon, badgering the bartender to pour one more on the house for the *real* Mikey, goddammit! He'll drink it! Mikey'll drink anything.

I speak from experience. Most of you don't know this, but I was a child star and I have kept it under wraps because I thought it might hurt my career as an adult. You probably don't recognize me with the goatee but, yes, I played the little red-headed girl Margaret on *Dennis the Menace*. Fuck you, Wilson!

The most miraculous thing about children—other than their uncanny ability to repeat verbatim in front of your boss every joke you've ever made about his speech impediment—is their innocence, their sweetness, and their utter, total trustfulness. Children truly do believe in the goodness of mankind. Throw a child into show business, a world where the phrase "I'll call you" actually means "I will use every ounce of will that I possess to avoid coming into contact with you for as long as the sun shines in the heavens and I continue to draw breath," and, trust me, that childlike quality will be stripped faster than a fully loaded Lexus parked in front of a Detroit crack house.

Christ, isn't it hard enough for a kid to have a normal child-hood without being schlepped around to audition for every walleyed, halitosistic, bad-toupeed, spits-when-he's-talking casting director in town? Putting your kid in show business means taking him to meet the very people you should be doing everything in your power to protect him from. The only idiots who don't see that are frustrated stage parents who try to fill their career-void by being so demonically driven they make William Randolph Hearst look like Jeff Spicolli.

Fortunately, you can tell when your kids are in danger of becoming child stars. There are some tea leaves you can read. Like if you tell them to go out and play, and they say, "Play how? Moody? Belligerent?" Or if your kid sees news coverage of another kid trapped in a well and says, "Hey, did I read for that?" Or if you call your kids in for dinner and they say, "Sorry, I don't eat with the crew." All of these are bad signs.

No child *really* wants to be in show business. Ask little kids what they want to be, and they'll say a fireman or an astronaut. I guarantee you, not one will say: "I want to be on a set all day with a bunch of alcoholic, prescription drug–addicted, psychotically self-involved adult costars, waiting to say my completely unrealistic lines that illustrate how adorably wise and precocious I am."

We all think our kids are adorable and say smart, funny things, and that the world would love them if it could just see them on the big screen. But that doesn't make them actors; it just makes us parents. If you honestly think any one kid is that much cuter than any other, you're missing the point. All kids are cute. They're designed that way. There is no such thing as a kid who isn't cute. The trick in parenting is to make sure your kids

A GOLDEN SHOWER OF PRAISE FOR TV

Did you watch any of the presidential debate coverage this year? Can you believe we winnowed down the race for the presidency to that bunch of jagoffs? You know, that was one good thing about having only three television stations way back in the early '50s—none of this debate shit would ever even have made it on TV. Maybe that's why they call it the Golden Age.

Now, I don't want to get off on a rant here, but when people talk about the Golden Age of Television, they're usually referring to TV in the early '50s. And while I admire much of that ephemeral genius, I think the Golden Age of Television had as much to do with timing as it did with inspiration, because you can only be first once. I mean, c'mon, nobody remembers his second blow job. Unless, of course, you kept the receipt—a jerk-off write-off.

In the '50s, TV was just starting to explore a future of infinite possibilities. Now it's all been done. A talking car? *Knight Rider* and *My Mother the Car*. A wacky space alien? *3rd Rock, Mork, Alf*. A talking chimp? *Lancelot Link* and . . . I.

Television of the early '50s featured ballet, opera, plays by Chayefsky. You know why? Because nobody was watching it back then. Once everyone decided it was time to start making a buck off the magic picture box, quality disappeared faster than Brian Dennehy hearing the words, "Here's your plate, the buffet table's over there."

There were problems in the 1950s. Advertisers ruled the roost, and they wanted no part of society's dark side. Consequently, there are many episodes of classic '50s television shows that have never been aired. Like the *Andy Griffith* episode "Otis Joins the Klan." Or the *Ozzie & Harriet* episode "Get a Job, You Lazy Fuck." Or the never-seen episodes of *I Love Lucy* entitled "I Love Lucy and Ethel," "I Love Lucy and Fred," "Fred and Ethel Love Lucy While I Watch," and, of course, the mega-controversial "I Love Lassie."

For me, the '50s weren't the Golden Age, because we didn't have remote control. When I was a kid, I was my family's remote control, getting up to change the goddamn channel every two seconds with a pair of needle-nosed pliers. Another reason I consider *today* to be the Golden Age of Television is that, with the advent of channel surfing, I haven't seen a commercial in the past ten years . . . except for the ones I'm in.

Truth be told, I'm kinda partial to the television being produced today. Remember that during the so-called Golden Age of the '50s, a lot of programming was just cheap, ratings-grabbing, big-money quiz shows that served as nonnutritious filler whenever the network wizards were out of original ideas. Thank God, current-day programmers don't see quiz shows as their final answer.

Sure, most television nowadays is crap. But guess what? Most television has always been crap. So has most film, music, painting, and literature, ever since the moment mankind started grinding it out. I'm sure there were cave-wall drawings of dogs playing poker. The old stuff that we see today seems extraordinary because it had to be, in order to survive. What we're seeing is what's made it through the cruelly discerning filter of time. Remember, for every Michelangelo's *David* there were hundreds of sculptures called *Naked Guy Hangin' Left*.

Maybe we're missing the point by even insisting that there was a Golden Age of Television. TV's value is in its ability to mirror our world, and to connect people instantly to whatever is taking place, real or not, on the screen. It's not meant to stand the test of time any more than David Caruso was meant to have a film career. When a show does hold up, it's a happy accident. I wish I had more to say but I don't, because right before the show tonight, my producer, Mel Cooley, told Buddy and Sally and me that my head writer tripped over a hassock that little Richie had left in the middle of the living-room floor, and his wife is leaving him to take a job at a newsroom in Minneapolis . . .

When I hear about the Golden Age of Television in the '50s, I have to think that that's akin to getting to first base and calling it quits. We are still exploring all that TV has to offer. Sure, some television was great then, but I also think it's really great now. Shows like *The Sopranos, Sex and the City, Oz, Chris Rock,* great documentaries, movies, boxing, Britney Spears specials . . . Somebody stop me before I ass-kiss myself into a fucking coma.

Of course, that's just my opinion. I could be wrong.

JOCKS WITHOUT CUPS

The U.S. Women's World Cup Soccer team is locked in a dispute about receiving the same compensation as the men's team. Can you believe we're busting these women's metaphorical balls over a few bucks after that incredible victory *in the World Cup finals*? Shouldn't we be paying them for taking the term "header" out of the White House and putting it back on the playing field, where it belongs?

Now, I don't want to get off on a rant here, but my topic today is "Women in Sports." I know what the women are thinking: oh, great, the goatee boy is gonna tell *us* about women in sports. We're gonna hear all about *women's* sports from the funny little man on TV who's more full of shit than a whale with no ass. Well, I happen to love women's sports. Sometimes even for the right reasons.

The increasing visibility of women's athletics has to be attributed to more than simply being the right idea at the right time. The Women's World Cup Soccer team and the players in the WNBA have struck a chord deep in the American psyche, because they have something that most pampered, overpaid, arrogant male athletes long ago forgot about: they have breasts—I mean, heart.

I believe the reason people follow women's sports nowadays is that, for the most part, female athletes are still pure. Women play for the reason male athletes used to play: the love of the game. They sure as hell aren't doing it for the money. Christ, the kids making their shoes are getting paid better than they are. When I read about male professional athletes being arrested for murder, assault, rape, and theft, I agree with those who say they just can't see women competing on the same level as men anytime in the near future.

As long as women have been around, they've had athletic ability. It's just that their defined role in our society was narrower than an armrest on Southwest Airlines. Opportunities for women used to be harder to come by than a PAT BUCHANAN FOR PRESIDENT button in a Mexican border town, but they are finally getting more plentiful. Our perception of female athletes has shifted from the clichéd lanky, deep-voiced, perpetually single, girls'-gym teacher to indisputably feminine sports figures like Mia Hamm, Gabrielle Reece, and Anna Kournikova. Although there are exceptions, like that Rodman chick. What's up with her?

If you doubt the genetic capability of women to physically compete with men, stay up late some night and check out women's bodybuilding on ESPN2. The other night I saw a woman who looked like a shiny fire hydrant with eyelashes, straining so hard in the final pose-down that a tiny, perfectly formed penis popped out of her bikini bottom. I've got some news for all you female bodybuilders out there, especially the ones who are more ripped than Hillary Clinton's love letters from Bill . . . people *are* checking you out, for the same reason they look at incredibly bad toupees. But no one is going to tell you that you look frightening, because we're all afraid you'll kick our scrawny little asses.

Female athletes must deal with a host of stereotypes, the most prominent being that women's sports is the exclusive domain of lesbians. Some people believe that LPGA stands for Look, Prick, Go Away. Like most stereotypes, that one is simply not true, except, of course, when it's true. I am not implying that there's anything wrong with lesbians, whether on the field or off, whether they're in training, or in the showers after the game, soaping each other's toned, hard bodies and giggling girlishly as their friendly pushing and teasing escalates into something much, much more . . . Where was I? Oh yeah, stereotypes. They're not true. Just not true. Maybe what's happening is that we've evolved to a point where we're no longer shoehorned into rigidly confined gender roles. Maybe we're developing into a society where it's okay for women to be forceful and powerful, competitive and driven, and it's okay for men to be soft and passive and do cross-stitch embroidery and cry at movies and squeal at kittens in baskets and walk around the house in their lacy underthings without their wives rolling their eyes and saying,

Alt.Medicine

GINGKO, SHMINKO!

For those of you who don't know what *yohimbé* is, join the club. I'm only familiar with gingko biloba, which, I believe, is the name of that city in Spain where that weird new art museum is. Now, I don't want to get off on a rant here, but is alternative medicine really the key to understanding the human body, or is it just a chance to get scammed by some loser who wasn't smart enough to snag the hair-scrunchie franchise at the local mall?

One major tenet of alternative medicine is "natural is good, synthetic is bad." This kind of thinking is more simplistic than the B-plot on an episode of *Nash Bridges*. While I don't believe traditional medicine has all the answers, it must be pretty frustrating for a Harvard-trained M.D. to be losing customers to a guy whose sole medical credential consists of preferring to sit on the floor. I divide medical practitioners into two camps. Those who will give me a scrip for Vicodin over the phone, and those who won't.

I have to admit that as cynical and untrusting by nature as I might be, I am becoming more open to experimenting with alternative medicines. I don't mean taking them myself, I mean recommending them to friends and neighbors so they'll take them and I can see if they really do work.

In college, my roommates and I experimented with alternative medicines—one guy would say "Howzabout some aromatherapy?" and then he would fart, and the other guy would say "Howzabout some reflexology?" and give him the finger. And, trust me, all the chicks really dug it when we'd wink and ask them if they'd like to come up to our dorm room for a little "Cock-u-pressure."

Since then, I've learned that there are many different kinds of alternative medicine, each based on different theories. For example, there's acupuncture, which works on the principle of distraction. You're not going to feel the arthritis in your knee when someone's ramming a butterfly-specimen needle into the nape of your neck. It's the same reason your nose never itches when your ankle is caught in a bear trap.

Another theory says that the key to good health is colonic irrigation. You all know what a colonic is, don't ya? It's when a trained professional puts eight quarters into the coin slot of a carwash pressure wand and details your interior. I decided I would give it a try, but my wife came home early and caught me power-squatting over her bidet like an orangutan with osteoporosis, and I had to sleep in the rec room until she got that sick little picture out of her head.

Maybe that made me a tad skeptical about alternative medicine. If I'm seeking treatment for something, I want documentation of my improvement. I want a guy in a lab coat showing me before-and-after X rays and test results charted on graph paper. What I don't want is my specialist basing his conclusion that I'm cured on the fact that his stepcousin Bobby Wasabi saw two doves fucking in a dream.

I don't think Western culture has all the answers, but it sure does seem like people in India flock to the Red Cross in droves whenever that tent pops up, huh? Hey—maybe that's *their* alternative medicine. Bottom line, the human body is a mysterious thing, and there's absolutely nothing wrong with exploring all the options available. Just remember, every once in a while, the untutored maverick the medical establishment assumes doesn't know what he's talking about . . . actually doesn't know what he's talking about.

Look, we're Americans—optimistic, addicted to the quick fix, constantly on the hunt for the new and exotic. It's much easier for us to accept a guy with a big white beard hawking his custom blend of saw palmetto and squirrel dandruff than it is to hear a real doctor tell us to lay off the Big Macs, get off our fat asses, and take a walk every decade or so.

If alternative medicine is so much better than mainstream science, then tell me this, Nick Natural. Where is your alternative medicine's magical tincture that allows me to stroll through a pollen-laden field of dandelions and still feel like I'm walking on sunshine? Where's your shark cartilage that allows me to start each morning with a stick of butter, a half-dozen Cinnabons, and a pot of espresso, without four o'clock rollin' around and me trying to figure out if I've just got gas or if it really is check-out time? And where's your enchanted cedar bark that makes my dick harder than a lasting Middle East peace? I'll tell you where it is, Vishnu. Traditional, mainstream, corporate-funded, evil Western medicine. That's where the fuck it is. Okay?

Of course, that's just my opinion. I could be wrong.

MINIMUM WAGES OF SIN

Why would anybody want to marry a complete stranger for their money? Well, I guess it beats workin'. Now, I don't want to get off on a rant here, but aside from gravity and how good it feels to put a Q-tip too far into your ear, nothing quite unites mankind like the fact that at one time or another, just about all of us have had a lousy job.

My grandfather always used to say, "Dennis," and about five minutes later, I'd say, "Yes, Grampa?" And then he'd say, "Dennis, always do something you love, and you'll never work a day in your life." Of course, my grandfather operated the hoof-grinder at a Hormel plant and he was extremely sarcastic, but it's a cute story. You would think that in this country nobody would have to settle for a bad job. Why, then, *why* would someone willingly subject themselves to an environment where they are constantly humiliated, degraded, and debased? The answer is quite simple: my writers have no green cards.

There are many ways to know that you have a bad job. For instance, if you have to carry out the body of the guy whose place you are taking. If you're employed at the post office next to a coworker who's constantly muttering under his breath and the only word you can ever make out is your first name. And, most important, you never want to be the bathroom attendant in an Indian restaurant.

The problem with bad jobs is that often they make you dress the part. Every time I go to the food court at a mall and see those girls at that lemonade-and-corndog place wearing the red hot-pants and the multicolored hats, I have to bite my tongue to keep from screaming, "Sell your blood!" I worked as an usher in a movie theater when I was a teenager. I had to wear black tuxedo pants, a white ruffled shirt, and a black bow tie, all topped off with a burgundy polyester jacket with the company crest over my left breast. Christ, I looked like a prom narc. You wanna be wearing formal attire when the guy whose dick you're shining a flashlight on looks up at you and says, "Pray for me?"

I've had lots of bad jobs. There was the Fotomat gig where a lady got testy because her pictures weren't there in twenty-four hours as promised. I tried to keep it together, but when she called me an incompetent minimum-wage slug, I told her I had to send her order back to the lab because the photographs of her ass wouldn't fit into the booth.

I have friends who have, in my opinion, the worst jobs anyone could possibly imagine, but they are either fucking with my head or completely insane because they think they've got life by the balls. My friend Joey cleans out the small-object filter screen at a major urban sewage treatment plant. He calls himself a "flow-facilitation engineer," and he insists that the job has many perks and often winks at me as he makes large purchases with buckets full of damp, stinky, loose change.

For twenty-five years my friend Cliff has scooped dead animals off country roads for a living. Cliff fancies himself a "pelt wrangler." He also insists that the rewards of his job go beyond the paycheck, as he casts a proud glance toward his fur-lined den, out of which he operates his all-natural, eyes-are-still-in-'em toupee business.

And then there's Lindell, who puts electronic surveillance ankle bracelets on people under house arrest. Lindell loves being part of the criminal justice system because he feels that too many people are immoral and unethical and, besides, from time to time a hooker will give him a hand job for loosening the bracelet a notch. The point I'm making is there's good work out there. But, more important, if your sense of who you are is entirely wrapped up in what you do for a living, I feel sorry for you. There is so much more to who a person is than how he collects a check. There's family. There's friends. There's hobbies. And, above all, there's going down to your local Subway shop and staring through the window at the guy your age in the canary-yellow "Sandwich Artist" polo shirt sweating over a provolone-and-salami hoagie like he's defusing a fucking bomb, and you thanking God that you are not him.

Of course, that's just my opinion. I could be wrong.

Revenge

I JUST CALLED TO SAY "FUCK OFF"

Now, I don't want to get off on a rant here, but revenge has been a basic human motivation since Noah sailed his ark past the drowning jerks who picked him last in high-school Phys Ed, and yelled, "Good luck on the swim team, fuckers."

Life as we know it is completely based on revenge. It all started with Adam and Eve being expelled from paradise for eating an apple. Does that not reveal to you a vengeful God? God likes vengeance. God encourages it. He's kicking people out of paradise for eating *apples*. Turns out, God is a touchy cosmic Korean grocer. Oh, and by the way, for those of you who are not of the Judeo-Christian persuasion, just think of revenge as "induced karma."

My general rule of thumb when it comes to revenge is to not give in to my first impulse to throw a punch. Primarily, that's because the only guy I can beat up had his birthday announced by Willard Scott this morning. But sometimes enough is enough. The other day I'm at Denny's, and I order two eggs and three silver-dollar pancakes. The waitress serves me *three* eggs and *two* silver-dollar pancakes. So, I very calmly whipped out a can of lighter fluid and torched the entire establishment, all the while whistling the tune "Disco Inferno."

Everybody's life is chock-a-block full of opportunities for retribution. The workplace, with all its shifting alliances and power plays, is a ripe setting. I have never peed in the boss's coffeepot but I have suggested that the coffee tastes salty and just winked at him. The death penalty is society's ultimate form of revenge, especially if you fake the guy out and make like you hear the phone ringing just before you throw the switch.

Even in what's passing today for our leaders, the urge for revenge festers like a clamhouse Dumpster on an August afternoon. Bush's entire presidential campaign was built on settling a score. His father lost to Bill Clinton in 1992, and he's still pissed. For eight years, George Senior was seething over his loss to that smirking, two-timing two-termer. Everybody knew it was only a matter of time before Bush Senior showed up on the parapet of the Texas governor's mansion like the ghost in *Hamlet*, screaming, "Avenge me, Dubya! Avenge me!"

I think our goal shouldn't be eradicating human beings' need for revenge as much as it should be refining it. Be creative. Ladies, you really want to get back at a man for dumping you, it's very simple: get his new girlfriend drunk and go to bed with her, then call him up and tell him how great she was. He'll simultaneously be so pissed off and insanely turned on that you'll short-circuit his brain and his dick in one vengeful masterstroke. By the way, if you do try that, please submit to me a meticulously detailed report on how it all turned out and a video.

So, summing up, just think of revenge as an indispensable release valve for an increasingly pseudocivilized society. These days, Americans feel they have only two options when someone has harmed them. They can beat the shit out of that person, or they can hire a lawyer. Hey, I got a better idea. Let's kill two birds with one stone. Next time somebody does you wrong, go beat the shit out of a lawyer.

Of course, that's just my opinion. I could be wrong.

God

HIGH AND MIGHTY PISSED

Whatever happened to the separation of Church and Hate? Now, I don't want to get off on a rant here but it's amazing how, in an election year, God's name gets thrown around like a drunken dwarf at a biker rally.

When I try to picture God, I always see some guy wearing a white robe and frantically working a huge panel of switches and knobs while answering prayers like a hopped-up Larry King taking phone calls. You know—"Columbia, South Carolina, go ahead . . . How many times do I have to tell you? Take that goddamn flag down. Now!"

Every religion has its own concept of God, and every religion is wrong. They have to be. We're talking about the ultimate totality here, and no one creed can have absolute dominion over its definition . . . Man, I wish I'd said that sophomore year when I was trying to do Brenda Wilkins. You know, I had *Dark Side of the Moon* on, we were splitting a bottle of Mateus, talking existentialism. If I had had this pseudophilosophical bullshit down back then, I would have gotten laid like Mothra's egg.

Western religions tend to imagine God as either a burning bush or Wilford Brimley with a beard and dreadlocks. In the East, you get a little more leeway: one god is a bare-breasted woman with six arms, another is a man with the head of an elephant. There is no doubt in my mind as to who had the better weed.

What happens to gods when people cease to worship them? Do they sit alone on Mount Olympus wondering what the fuck Harry Hamlin was doing in *Clash of the Titans,* or do they descend to earth and take jobs as wisecracking hosts of late-night cable talk shows? And I've saideth too much . . .

The concept of God lets you imagine there's something more, that when you die, you stumble out of this demented funhouse and there's someone there to explain what the hell you just went through, like the epilogue on a Quinn Martin show. That's all I want—I want everything clarified, do you hear me, God? *Everything*. I want a perfectly logical reason for all the wars, shootings, tortures, rapes, murders, cruelty, and pain. And when You're done with that, can you please explain the frogs in *Magnolia*?

Even though Jesus once admonished, "Render unto Caesar what is Caesar's," God and commerce do frequently overlap.

Did you ever notice the phrase "In God We Trust" only appears on the lesser denominations of our currency? You get up to the thousand-dollar bill, and it just says "God, I Think I Can Take It from Here."

I don't think there's any doubt that people often yell "Oh God" during sex because He wants to be appreciated for his best invention. If you don't shout His name when smelling a rose, well, that's okay. Not really bowled over by the sight of a glorious sunset? Fair enough. But if you don't give Him his props for orgasms that make your toes curl like frying bacon, well, you're about to feel the awesome wrath of the Almighty's lightning-bolt enema up your ass.

Yes, some of God's handiwork is flawed. There are rivers that overflow, volcanoes that aren't quite sealed, and tectonic plates that tend to crack over time. But isn't it comforting to know that even God has trouble finding a reliable contractor? And for someone who is so great and all-powerful, God's got an awful lot of people talking for him these days, doesn't he? God's got more phonies claiming to know His will than Howard Hughes. Jerry Falwell says homosexuality and abortion are sins. Yeah, well, so is gluttony, Jerry, so why don't you drop about fifty pounds or so?

Don't get me wrong. People are entitled to worship as they see fit, but don't go using God as a convenient template for all your petty, bigoted views. If you want to ban interracial dating at the college you preside over because your father once caught you masturbating to a picture of Pam Grier and punished you by making you paint the house, and now every time you smell wet

DuPont Latex Exterior it makes you think of Foxy Brown and you get all confused and horny and humiliated at the same time and you want to make someone pay, just fucking say so, okay? Don't put it on God.

Of course, that's just my opinion. I could be wrong.

Patriotism

OF THEE I SNARL

When you see the people in Taiwan—or anywhere else for that matter—having free elections, it makes you proud that we invented modern democracy. God, I love this country. Now, I don't want to get off on a rant here, but while I am cynical toward politics and government in general, I am a patriot through and through. I love this country for several reasons, not the least of which is that I know I'm allowed to hate it if I want to. I've been patriotic for a long time. I wasn't quite old enough to be drafted into the army during the Vietnam War, but had I been, you can rest assured that I would have used an American rifle to shoot myself in the foot.

I hate it when foreigners come to America and start bad-mouthing this place. Because that's *my* job. We are a nation that celebrates our Independence Day by barbecuing ourselves into a hot-link-kielbasa coma, but patriotism, my fellow Americans, should be an around-the-clock, twelve-months-a-year job.

When it comes to fostering patriotism, we have always depended on the unkindness of strangers, countries like Germany, Russia, and Iran. And trust me—we need our enemies. I mean, without Bluto, Popeye's just a vegetarian sailor who likes anorexic chicks.

But my problem with patriotism is that often it's all too easy. Where's the challenge in saying that you're proud to be an American? Of course you love this place. All you have to do is watch the nightly news to thank the Lord that we don't live anywhere else. We should be flying the Stars and Stripes every day just for not living in a country with barefoot soldiers, insane heat, flat breads, and giant banners with a pockmarked, beret-wearing leader's picture on them.

God bless America! And God bless the Caymans, where I have most of my offshore accounts.

Of course, that's just my opinion. I could be wrong.

The Penis

SCHLONG'S DAY JOURNEY INTO NIGHT

Now, I don't want to get off on a rant here, but you may have heard the penis called many things: the flesh crank, the one-eyed monster, peacemaker, schwantz, third leg, Rumpleforeskin, or, if you're like me, you've simply heard it called "the Munchkin log."

I love my penis. Not love as in "I love *The Sopranos*" but love as in "I love air." Dick, Prick, Prong, Dong. Call it what you will, it is My locus / My focus / My wand of hocus-pocus / The petals on my crocus / "Be careful! It might soak us!" See? What other organ can make a man leap into a giddy rhyme like that? None. Because for a man, the penis is the wellspring of his joy. Remember, two-thirds of happiness is 'piness.

Mankind has always been obsessed with the penis. Sigmund Freud is the father of modern penis thought. He invented the phrase "phallic symbol." Before Freud, people would look at a tower or a pine tree and say, "I love it. I wish I knew why . . ."

Guys, enjoy your penis while you can, because eventually you'll summon it to the center ring, and it will remain docile in its cage. And any guy who thinks that lost erections are the only penile dysfunctions coming down the pike hasn't stood at a urinal in a public restroom next to some old guy who's shaking it like he's rolling dice to spare the life of a loved one.

I felt pretty good when they said the average penis is about six inches. Then I found out that in coming up with that figure, they factored in women. But size is less important to women than we tend to think it is. As visually stimulating as it may be, I don't think the average gal wants to risk pelvic injury with some two-liter-Pepsi-bottle-sized freak whose idea of foreplay is hooking up an extra quart of blood to his arm so he can get hard without passing out.

So, if women don't care, why do guys obsess about size? Well, guys like easily quantifiable measurements like length or girth, while women treasure more abstract qualities, like emotional maturity or kindness. Admittedly, I'm generalizing here. Some guys do value maturity and kindness. They're called "guys with tiny dicks."

I guess it's not surprising, but penis-enlargement surgery is rapidly growing in popularity. For about six thousand dollars, you can gain about an inch in length. That seems ridiculous to me. I mean, for five bucks you can just get condoms with vertical stripes. Saw that on Martha Stewart . . . My advice if you're considering penile lengthening: take your time and put some thought into it. Then pick a reputable doctor from the ads in the sports section of your town's second-best newspaper.

On the off-chance you think your penis is too big, you needn't suffer either. Just grow your pubic hair extra long so that your penis looks smaller. I rub a bottle of Rogaine into my pubic hair every night, and now my genitals look like Gene Shalit smoking a tiparillo.

The happiest I ever was with my penis was in the years leading up to the eleventh grade, which is when I had the misfortune of having gym class with Duncan Loomis. Duncan Loomis was a pimply kid about five foot six, 137 pounds, 37 pounds of which was pure cock. Duncan Loomis was a lousy athlete, so he'd spend the entire gym class asking, "Is it time to hit the showers, Coach?" Because the showers is where Duncan Loomis was king. I had the locker next to his, and when he took off his jockstrap, which, by the way, his mother had reinforced with the webbing used on the outdoor patio furniture, I swear to God, there was an audible whoosh as he flopped it out, and a discernible gust of wind that was capable of blowing all our hair back. And, quite frankly, when you stood him next to me, we were like a before-and-*never* advertisement. Then he'd wrap a towel around his waist in such a way that his massive tool was nudging through the opening like an elephant's trunk searching out peanuts from the back of a circus tent, and he'd saunter through the locker room like Gulliver, surveying the sad crop of Lilliputian nubs on the poor cursed mortals before him as he laughed and bellowed, "Behold the glory of Duncan Loomis!!!"

By the way, I saw Duncan Loomis at my last high-school re-union, and his wife had a tired smile and a funny walk.

Of course, that's just my opinion. I could be wrong.

SATAN'S LITTLE HELPERS

Now, I don't want to get off on a rant here, but let's face it—we all have a dark side. Of course, some people are more inherently evil than others. For lack of a better word, let's just call them . . . Germans. But deep down we know that every one of us is capable of going ballistic given the right set of emotional launch codes.

Man is at constant odds with his demons, but you can't beat a demon, because demons don't fight fair. The only way to keep a demon at bay is to love your demon. Take your demon out to lunch, get your demon a little tipsy, cop a feel off your demon, and then go back to the demon office and tell all the other demons around the demon cooler that your demon puts out like a demon.

The news broadcasts tales from the dark side every night in living color. How can we allow ourselves to derive morbid pleasure from watching NATO airstrikes, with the Dow Jones industrial average scrolling across the bottom of the screen, no less? It must be the same switch in our brain that we turn off when we boil a lobster or, worse yet, tell a lobster that the yellow twist-ties on its claws mean that it's Mardi Gras. Unfortunately, evil is perversely compelling. It always has been. Let's face it, the Bible is duller than operating instructions for a hinge—until the snake shows up.

We are all embroiled in a daily struggle against the darker forces in our lives, like greed, selfishness, and dishonesty. I'm no exception. I'm a slave to my own interests. The other day I'm downtown, washing the feet of the homeless like I do every Wednesday, and suddenly I remember that it's my turn to bake cookies for the guys over at the firehouse but I also promised the school-bus driver, Maddie, that I'd fill in for her that afternoon so she could take her kid to the doctor. So, double-quick I rinse off Big Rudy, check his bunion, and hurry home. But there's a squirrel in my driveway, and he's unconscious and his leg's broken, so I have to give him mouth-to-mouth and make him a splint, and then there's no time to bake my famous truffled chocolate-macadamia bars from scratch, so I cut corners and I use a mix and, to make matters even worse, I lie and tell the firemen that I *did* make them from scratch. See? I'm a bad, bad man.

I'm not saying we should all strip naked and smear ourselves with goat's blood while running for the presidency on the Re-form Party ticket, but it is liberating, indeed, even therapeutic, to occasionally dip your little toe into the bracing waters of the verboten. The purveyors of mass culture understand this and provide us with a never-ending stream of reasonably safe thrills to give our sometimes humdrum lives a sanitary, socially acceptable jolt. Slasher movies, Clive Barker novels, a backstage camera at the VH1 "Divas Live" concert, all are the mental equivalent of a temporary "Hell's Angels" tattoo: a round-trip ticket allowing us a noncommittal sortie into the realm of the aberrant.

The truth nobody wants to admit is that we need the concept of evil because it makes good look so much more attractive by contrast. It's the same reason jewelers always show diamonds against black velvet. You can't have heroes if you don't have villains. Without Hitler, there is no Churchill. Without Saddam Hussein, there is no Colin Powell. Without Crabtree, there is no Evelyn. And without Darth Vader, well, Luke Skywalker's just another hotshot rocketsled jockey in white jammies hittin' on his sister.

Of course, that's just my opinion. I could be wrong.

Education

SCHOOLS FOR
SCANDAL

They say that since *Who Wants to Be a Millionaire* came on, there's a renewed thirst for knowledge in this country. It's kind of unfortunate though that Regis Philbin turns out to be the one who leads us to drink from the fountain of wisdom, rather than some of the incredibly dedicated teachers in this country. Now, I don't want to get off on a rant here, but I think we have a problem when the people we hire to be guards at schools are making more than the teachers we pay to educate our kids.

I think it speaks volumes about how little we value basic education in America that only one of the Three R's actually begins with the letter "R."

I love my kids' teachers, but sometimes parent/teacher conferences can have a nuclear weapons–summit level of intensity because every problem Junior has can be blamed on someone in that room. That's why I always go to my conferences wearing army fatigues that I soaked in gin the night before. That way, the teacher thinks my kids are doing pretty damn good, considering.

Teachers are said to have a high rate of stress and burnout. If you are a teacher, there are signs you may be at risk. For example, if rather than try to remember the names of your students you refer to them all as "Fucko." Or, more than once a week you find yourself saying, "Try me, dipshit." Or if you've invented a new game for your class called "Throw the Scissors Hard."

Nearly every high-school teacher falls into one of a handful of basic categories. There's Tough-but-Fair, who is universally feared and respected by the freaks and the straights alike. Tough-but-Fair doesn't give much homework because he can't be bothered grading it, but at the start of each term assigns a reading list that would make Susan Sontag cry. Every few years, a student inevitably asks him why *he's* never written a book, whereupon the classroom grows uncomfortably silent while Tough-but-Fair clenches his jaw muscles and stares out the window for a long time, then mutters, "Guess I just never got around to it," and gives a surprise quiz on the complete works of Thomas Pynchon. Nobody ever asks him a personal question again.

The next teacher type is Best Friend. Best Friend insists that you call her by her first name, and addresses the class as "People." She's everyone's favorite teacher, for the obvious reason that her total lack of authority makes her an easy mark and also because her insistence that everyone move their chairs into a circle at the start of class is good for wasting at least half a period. If Best Friend knew what her students said about her behind her back, she would never stop crying.

My favorite teacher by far, though, is Tenure Jockey. Old, cranky, and shuffling, Tenure Jockey is permanently stooped, ground down by serving under decades of monolithic academic bureaucracy. He wears the same tweed jacket with suede patches at the elbows every single day and smells like cherry pipe tobacco and defeat. His Xeroxed handouts are always missing the top or bottom third of the page, and he hasn't altered his lesson plan since Huey Long was shot. And you know what the really frightening part is? When I was in Tenure Jockey's class, he seemed so ancient and decrepit, but he was probably younger than I am right now.

Whatever types of teacher we're talking about, they all have one thing in common: they are grossly underpaid. Somehow, we must convince all Americans that paying teachers what they deserve is as good an investment in our future as, say, building more prisons. Okay, maybe compensating teachers fairly is out of the question, because society realizes that we've got them by the short hairs. They *need* to be teachers, and as is often the case in this country, when we know somebody loves to do something, we fuck them over on their paycheck, because we figure they're going to do it anyway. But at least let them keep what little we're giving them. I know I wouldn't be where I am if it weren't for dedicated teachers honing my mind to a keen edge, and I say they should pay no taxes. If you're a math teacher grossing

$28,000 a year, and you have to pay zero percent in taxes, that means your take-home pay is . . . Uhhh . . . Well, whatever it is, it's good.

Bottom line: being a teacher today is more challenging than doing bikini waxes on Russian women. You enter your place of employment by passing through a metal detector that's beeping like the Roadrunner with Tourette's syndrome, and then spend six hours a day trying to drill even a subatomic-sized kernel of knowledge into the *Dawson's Creek*-and-Sony-Playstation-addled noggins of two dozen eye-rolling, world-weary, body-pierced felons-in-training who regard you with all the respect they would a stewardess on a spring-break charter flight to Cancún. And you know something? When you're not teaching kindergarten, it's even worse.

Of course, that's just my opinion. I could be wrong.

Friendship

PAL DENNY

Now, I don't want to get off on a rant here, but what is a friend? Usually a friend is someone with whom you have a lot in common, but sometimes opposites attract. For instance, one of my closest buddies is a wisecracking, cynical, self-centered prick with *blond* hair.

In a nutshell, a friend is someone who can see through your external surface bullshit to the deeper and more profound bullshit that lies within all of us. A friend is someone who, when you ask what he paid for his house, doesn't pull that it-was-so-long-ago-I-really-can't-remember shit. You ask him and he gives you a fucking number.

A sign that someone is a *great* friend is when I can go long stretches in his company without saying so much as a word. That's trust. My best friend? Actor John Garfield's perfectly preserved corpse.

Friends are so important that, if kids can't find real ones, they'll make them up. I remember in the eighth grade when this girl had to be excused from class—I overheard her tell the teacher that she got her "friend." I kept thinking to myself, "Boy, that must be a great friend if they can get you out of class." The next day, math class was getting pretty boring, so I told the nun I needed to go home because I got *my* "friend," but instead of letting me go she turned her college ring into her palm and hit me on the top of the skull so hard that to this day her college uses my head as a mold to make its rings.

Women will often say that it's a test of friendship when both of them like the same guy, but I don't think that has to be a problem. Most guys would be happy to sleep with both of them at once. I'm surprised more women don't pursue this solution. I guess, deep down, they just aren't committed to making their friendships work.

Sure, friendship is risky. When you let someone into your life, give them your trust and avail yourself of theirs, you open yourself up to the possibility of being hurt. But what's the alternative? Being a cold and distant emotional hermit whose only interest is himself? That's no way to live . . . unless, of course, you happen to make a shitload of money, in which case it'd be pretty damn sweet, because as we all know, you don't need friends if you have money.

Of course, that's just my opinion. I could be wrong.

Elvis

MEMPHIS SLIM
. . . OR FAT

Prince is the kind of rock-and-roll star we're stuck with today. Man, do I long for the days of the King. Now, I don't want to get off on a rant here, *ma'am*, but from his lean and hopeful beginnings to his sad and bloated end, Elvis Aaron Presley's life story fits our criteria for mythos and allegory like a skintight, jewel-encrusted, pit-stained, white leather jumpsuit.

Elvis blew the lid off the sexually repressed, uptight '50s, set the stage for the upheavals of the '60s, and *was* the excesses of the '70s. Elvis lives in our consciousness as icon, cautionary tale, alter ego, and punch line, embodying a litany of contradictions: a great talent with a boundless capacity for schlock, a transcendent live performer who starred in some of the most godawful movies known to man, a rebel who willingly served his country, and, most enigmatically, a man who liked white gravy *on top of* his brown gravy.

According to the biographers, Elvis was a big eater from the beginning of his life to the end. It's just that in his twenties he had the metabolism to burn all those calories off. When I was in my twenties, I ate six cheeseburgers a day and drank three quarts of buttermilk too, but instead of launching into a successful career as an international superstar, I used up the calories jerking off in my bedroom. Different paths. No regrets.

How big an Elvis fan am I? Just ask my sons, Tuinol and Seconal Miller. When Elvis first appeared on *The Ed Sullivan Show,* they had to shoot him from the waist up because CBS felt America wasn't ready for the gyrating pelvic thrusts of a hormonally crazed banshee. Pretty much the same reason CBS to this day insists that Dan Rather never come out from behind his desk.

Highbrow music critics always looked down their noses at Elvis, but he had much in common with history's greatest composers. Like Mozart, Elvis was a performer whose energy and stage presence brought him fame at a young age. And like Dvořák, Elvis synthesized African-American tonal idioms with European performance tradition. And most striking of all, Elvis and Johann Sebastian Bach were both deeply religious men who wrote chamber works for the Margrave of Brandenburg that were virtual textbooks of late baroque-era polyphonic counterpoint. Also, Presley and Bach: both monster pussy hounds.

Elvis is the most important musical force of the past hundred years. Look around. You don't see any Beatles impersonators, do you? Except for Oasis. Incidentally, ever notice all the Elvis impersonators portray him in that '70s blue sequined painkiller haze? It's a lot easier to impersonate *that* Elvis than the raw, sexually primed Elvis of the 1950s. In fact, nobody does Elvis from the '50s because they can't. After the '50s, even Elvis couldn't do Elvis and he pretty much became the world's highest-paid Elvis impersonator.

Is Elvis still alive? No, he isn't. If he was alive, he would have showed up and stopped his kid from marrying Michael Jackson . . . You know, even though he's *dead,* I'm shocked he didn't show up to put the kibosh on that freak show.

Elvis still exerts a mystical pull on all of us. An estimated 700,000 visitors file through Graceland each year. Put another way, that's nearly 800,000 teeth. How tastelessly did he decorate Graceland? It's like if the guy who put *The Price Is Right* showcases together was blind. Elvis bought shit for his home that's so hideous they won't even sell it in the Graceland giftshop. I've seen black velvet paintings of Jesus in clown makeup playing poker with dogs and big-eyed kittens that are less tacky.

Was Elvis a musical force of nature, a bridge between two cultural heritages, or just a lucky hick who stumbled into the right recording studio at the right moment in history? The answer is the same one Elvis might have given when confronted with the five-page menu from Skeeter's International House of Waffles and Deep-Fried Arterial Plaque House . . . "I'll have all of the above, ma'am, with a side order of more."

In summing up about Elvis, let me say this before I leave the building. When the post office made us vote for which Elvis stamp we wanted, I voted for fat Elvis and I was really disappointed when he didn't win. Any country can put out a stamp with a trim, young, sexy star on it, but to be a citizen of a land that proudly sticks on its mail an overweight, reclusive, constipated, pill-addicted, television-shooting, two-pounds-of-bacon-at-one-sitting, goddamn American *legend* . . . I think the King would have wanted it that way.

Of course, that's just my opinion. I could be wrong.

ANYTHING HE CAN DO, SHE CAN DO BETTER

Now, I don't want to get off on a rant here, but would I vote for a woman president? Yes, but only a woman who's had saline breast implants, not silicone, because that shows sound judgment.

Most men are intimidated by powerful women, so the idea of a female president is threatening to them. Women have to tread very carefully so as not to shatter fragile male egos, so my recommendation to the first serious female presidential candidate is that her campaign slogan should be "Oh. My God, You're So Big." When I hear that, I want to pull my lever.

All the old sexist arguments against a woman president have been shot down by . . . uh, ironically, men. Women are too emotional? Hey, we had a guy in the White House for eight years who teared up more easily than Fiona Apple slicing onions while watching *Old Yeller*. You say women aren't self-reliant enough? Three words: George W. Bush. Women aren't knowledgeable enough about the world? See above. Women are ruled by their biology? For chrissake, a red-assed monkey masturbating at the zoo is in more control of his impulses than three-quarters of Congress. And, lastly, women are too shallow, too concerned with frilly fashions and feminine makeup? Yes, I suppose those are traits best left out of the Oval Office, because they're much more suited for the head of the fucking FBI!

I think we will see a female president in the not-too-distant future, but, unfortunately, not until the powers that be have debased the office to the point where it's completely irrelevant.

How exactly do you get a woman into the Oval Office? You know, other than sneaking her in through the Rose Garden while the first lady's out of town . . . Well, first we need to create a climate conducive to a female presidency: the complete subjugation of all men. That's right, sisters. Lesbo Nation.

Seriously, for us to elect a woman president, we must get away from all the Venus-and-Mars bullshit and accept women as individuals, each with her own strengths and weaknesses. Could a woman act coolly and decisively in the event of a national crisis? It depends on the woman. Madeline Albright? Yes. Jennifer Tilly? No . . . And I *like* Jennifer Tilly.

Maybe we need a woman in the White House precisely because there hasn't been one there. Women have been excluded from that calculated minuet of back-scratching and palm-greasing that passes for leadership these days in Washington. Maybe it will take someone who's not entrenched in the political system to stub out the tobacco industry, pistol-whip the NRA, and make the public schools fit places for our kids.

We need more women in politics. Take a look at C-SPAN sometime. There are more gravy spots on Strom Thurmond's tie than there are women in Congress. If you're a woman, there's no way you can look at these rich, white, entitled, scotch-drinking, secretary-chasing old-school hacks and not feel more left out than Alan Greenspan at the Billy Bob Thornton–Angelina Jolie wedding reception.

And if we elect a woman president who turns out to be a corrupt, ineffectual, mediocre leader or, worse still, a total fuck-up who runs this country into the ground, well, guess what, ladies? Then, and only then, you will finally have achieved true equality.

Would I vote for a woman president? Hey, I would vote for a woman, a black, a Jew, a Hispanic, an Indian, or any combination thereof no matter what their politics because I'm so sick of the numbing sameness of the political landscape. I'd vote for absolutely anybody if it meant I wouldn't have to watch another pasty-faced glad-hander trying to look like a man of the people at an Appalachian sawmill by changing in the back of his limo from wing tips and a power suit into Ugg Boots and Dockers.

Of course, that's just my opinion. I could be wrong.

A PREMIUM SCREWING

With all these assholes out there suing for the slightest indignity, you really need to have an umbrella insurance policy these days. Being in the smartass business, I've got higher premiums than a Chicago gas station. Now, I don't want to get off on a rant here, but how do you know you are getting screwed by your insurance company? Well, do you have an insurance company? Then you're getting screwed.

Insurance is a uniquely modern atrocity. At the dawn of man, there was no insurance. You either lived or died. There was no fast-grunting biped called "Homo Deductus" demanding a piece of your meat every month to guarantee that your fire wouldn't go out.

Buying insurance is a total pain in the ass. You have to sit there listening to some fear-pimp in an ill-fitting Sears King's Road Edition suit and a clip-on tie, who's more persistent than Keith Richard's morning cough, as he shuffles through papers he keeps in a battered briefcase with a SHIT HAPPENS sticker on it and recites worst-case scenarios in hushed, melodramatic tones like a sadistic older brother telling ghost stories just before bedtime. As a matter of fact, that's how they always end their sales pitch . . . "and all he had left was a bloody stump . . . Anyway, I'll just let you folks sleep on this and call you tomorrow. 'Night now."

The whole thing makes no sense, and the only thing that makes less sense is the actual policy. My auto insurance coverage is so elaborately worded, it makes the warranty on a dialysis machine read like *The Velveteen Rabbit*. As a result, I end up paying hefty auto insurance premiums so that when my parked car gets hit by some nearsighted Señor Magoo who's in this country illegally, has no insurance, and is driving with a learner's permit because he failed his driving test four times, since he's not used to paved roads, and he sues *me,* claiming back injury, soft-tissue damage, and emotional distress, my goddamn rates go up and they make him president of the fucking insurance company.

Health insurance is another muddled mess. When you go to a doctor for a physical, it quickly becomes apparent that the level of care you're going to receive is in direct correlation to the quality of your insurance. Years ago I had a medical policy with less coverage than an Alan-Keyes-for-president press conference, from a questionable insurance company called "Jimmy's

What're-You-Callin'-Me-For House of Bad Paper." As soon as the receptionist saw that, she told me to sit on the floor and not touch any of the *new* magazines. The physical itself? Well, the doctor tested my reflexes by unexpectedly punching me really hard in the stomach. And then he refused to check my prostate but said he'd talk me through it if I wanted to do it myself.

If you have a family, you must have some insurance to protect them in case something happens to you. For example, if I ever have to tongue-kiss Don Knotts on TV, my family gets three million dollars. The premiums are killing me, but at least I can sleep at night. As the breadwinner in my household, I also think it's a good idea to have life insurance. But, I have to admit, there's something about the postmortem payday that feels so, so wrong. We're talking about my death here! The end of Me. Call me selfish, but I want to be missed, and something about that Allstate Prize Van pulling up the driveway . . . like it's the Comedian's Clearinghouse Lottery . . . Well, that's gonna cut the edge off the grief right there, huh?

The worst part of the insurance business is that it's finite. Once everyone in America has bought policies covering their life, health, and property, if the insurance companies want to keep making money, they've gotta keep coming up with stuff to scare people with. So what's next? Insurance against boring parties, or bad dates, or disillusionment about how our lives turned out? I'd like reimbursement if I go to a concert and some lame '70s band decides not to play their one fucking hit song, or if my presidential candidates make me go to sleep faster than a hamster swimming in a bucket of Thorazine. And, of course, given how tightfisted those assholes in Hartford, Connecticut, are, if something catastrophic happens and you ever want to see a dime, you'd sure as shit better have some insurance insurance.

Folks, it all comes down to symbolism. You gotta love the symbols that the insurance companies use to convey protection: Allstate has the open hands, Traveler's has the umbrella, Nationwide has a blanket. Until you try to file a claim—then they all have the same symbol: a big, knobby eight-inch dildo. Actually, it's a ten-inch dildo, but there's a two-inch deductible.

Of course, that's just my opinion. I could be wrong.

THAT NEW-CAR STENCH

Now, I don't want to get off on a rant here but I just purchased a new car and let me tell you, it was a fantastic experience. I go down to the dealership and I'm greeted by Karmoosh, a go-getting young immigrant from some country whose flag depicts an American being shot. I don't want to say the guy was full of shit, but in the hour and a half I was with him, he showed me more faces than a mythological Hydra staring into a disco ball.

A car dealership is a special circle of Hell, a septic tank of desperation, suspicion, and loathing. The customers hate the dealers, the dealers hate the customers, the salespeople are all in competition with each other, and everyone assumes everyone else is lying. That new-car smell? Nothing more than the purest distillation of basic human contempt.

But not all the news is bad. One relatively recent innovation in car-buying is haggle-free pricing. They use this system with Saturns. And you know why? Because no one wants to buy a Saturn.

And then there's the leasing option. Leasing is just like buying, only instead of you giving the dealer money so you can own the car, you give the dealer money so *he* can own the car. I talked to a lot of dealers, and they ALL seem to *really* like this option.

When you go to buy a car, you are passed around from salesman to salesman like an apple bong at a Jimmy Page concert, so the first thing you want to do is keep the salesperson a little off-balance. Be courteous and pleasant to the point of almost appearing oblivious, and maybe even a little stupid. Then go for a test drive. Very important: you must take control of the test drive early. Otherwise, you've got the dealer yakking away while he's fiddling with the stereo, trying to guess what kind of music you dig so the two of you can "band-bond." To prevent this, before the test drive even begins, slip on a pair of Italian-leather racing gloves and request that you be accompanied by a salesman who doesn't have any children. Then ask for a helmet. As you're putting the helmet on—sideways—look at the guy through the earhole and say, "Boy, these cars have sure changed a lot since the last time I broke out." And, most important, during the test drive, always refer to the car as a "Nasty Bitch," as in the following sentences, "What kind of gas mileage does this nasty bitch get?" "Hey, does this nasty bitch come in blue?"

If buying a new car is akin to a seven- to ten-year stay in a Turkish prison, then buying a used car is akin to a seven- to ten-year stay in a Turkish prison in Alabama. The last time I was in the market for a used car I found myself checking out a lime-green '76 Dodge Aspen with a peeling white vinyl top, two missing hubcaps, and the words EXTRA SHARP!!, SPORTY, and LADY DRIVEN hand-painted on the windshield. Soon, I was met with a cheerful "Howdy there" by a man whose name, I would later learn from court documents, was Ronnie Sweet. Fifty years old, with an out-of-a-bottle tan lending his skin the healthy glow of a circus peanut, Ronnie was topped off by an immaculate Conway Twitty–style pompadour that reminded me of an Ocean Spray label, offset by nose hairs so unkempt it looked like he had just inhaled Bob Marley, feet first. Ronnie had white patent-leather side-zipper demiboots shined to the point where the reflection was summoning magi in search of the Christ child. To say Ronnie was a talker is like saying Jimi Hendrix knew a few chords. In the space of about five minutes, I was in and out of his "office," which consisted of a small U-Haul trailer hitched to the back of a perpetually idling Cadillac, and I had traded nine-hundred-ninety-nine of my hard-earned dollars for a set of disturbingly rusty keys and the haunting admonition: "It runs a little hot, and the muffled voice in the trunk is a fucking liar."

Face it, in America, cars have always been a status symbol and that puts the advantage squarely in the dealer's court. Most people walk into a dealership salivating about driving out with their dream ride, and salesmen prey on that neediness like a hawk swooping down on a limping field mouse. Buying a car is much like getting strapped into an unstoppable ass-fucking machine, so just make sure you sign on for the optional lubrication package.

Of course, that's just my opinion. I could be wrong.

Big Government

TIME TO TIGHTEN
THE BELTWAY

Due to high gas prices, Congress is considering temporarily dropping the federal gasoline excise tax. Hmmm . . . What's wrong with this picture? No doubt the lobbyists who buy the jet fuel to send our representatives on junkets to the Caribbean have been bitching about high prices . . .

To call our government a cesspool of waste is to do a disservice to all the plucky amoeba out there who thrive on human excrement. Now, I don't want to get off on a rant here, but I believe in downsizing government. I just don't know if it can be accomplished. Government is an immense, living, breathing monolith, and trying to cut any part of it away is like trying to trim a Great Dane's toenails when he's horny. I want a president who, like a Dodge City blacksmith, immediately begins shoveling white-hot coals under the deadweight lead-asses of Congress, pours off the slag, and beats whatever's left into a shiny platter upon which will sit the head of any future pork-barrel parasite who tries to get federal funding for a Goiter Museum in his home district.

If you want to put an end to government spending, it's very simple. Don't pay our president, senators, and representatives a salary. They say they can cut government spending; fine. Give them 10 percent of our tax refunds each year. If we did that, trust me, in three months the entire federal bureaucracy would be run out of a windowless basement in Georgetown by a ninety-year-old guy named Frankie with an unlisted rotary-dial phone.

I advocate a plastic-surgery approach. Lipo the fat out from where there's ugly excess and pump it back in where it's needed for a more pleasing effect. I get cross-eyed with rage when I hear that there are thirty-five students in a third-grade inner-city public-school class sharing one textbook while the AV-squad jerkoffs at NASA have lost contact with yet another billion-dollar piece-of-shit Radio Shack transmitter that was supposed to land on the surface of Mars and broadcast back pictures that I could take in Barstow in July. Hey, NASA. The space race is over. We *won*. We know all about space. It's full of black holes that relentlessly suck in all matter around them. Kind of like what you do with *our fucking money*. There might be water on Mars? Call me when you find oil on Mars, okay?

So where do we cut? Our government has branched out to keep pace with changing times, and that's fine, but we need to start pruning back the Federal Tree of Life. For example, what does the Department of the Interior do? They manage parkland. Yeah? So does my gardener. They're gone. Department of Energy? Gas prices are two bucks a gallon right now, they can be two bucks without these jagoffs. Gone. National Endowment for the Arts? Great artists don't need the government's money. Just ask Van Gogh. Okay, bad example. Anyway, the NEA? Gone. Health Department? I'm healthy. Gone.

Anyone who's ever called in a change of address to the post office knows that our government has about as much chance of ever becoming a lean, efficient machine as John Rocker has of getting a street named after him in Harlem. I say, don't just downsize government—get rid of it. You want to see an economically sound, well-run country, privatize the whole shooting match. We have the Staples Center and Qualcomm Stadium. Why not the Coca-Cola White House or the Home Depot Supreme Court? I mean, it's not like we already don't have the Smith & Wesson House of Representatives and the Philip Morris Senate.

Of course, that's just my opinion. I could be wrong.

ALL THE DISCOMFORTS OF HOME

I went on a vacation to Vietnam last year. Me loved it long time . . . They had *so* many German tourists over there, and they all had cameras. I guess Germans are so reflexively guilty about their past they now feel the need to document their every move in case they end up in front of some tribunal. In fact, it seems like every traveler is a little Abraham Zapruder today. You know the type, they spend the entire vacation with their right eyeball buried so deep inside the viewfinder of their video camera that when they finally do put the thing down, they look like Peter Falk with his balls caught in his zipper.

Now, I don't want to get off on a rant here, but travel lets us leave behind our unrealistic prejudices about other places and the people who live there and develop new, more realistic prejudices based on their actual deficiencies.

I hate travel so much I actually look forward to the day we can simply get in a transporter room and rematerialize at our desired location. If there's a molecular foul-up and I'm reconstituted wrong on the other side, that's okay.

And, come to think of it, what's the point of even traveling anymore? The world has become so homogenized that the only way you can tell what country you are in is by the language on the McDonald's menu. You find what you think is a virginal and untouched out-of-the-way land and I guarantee you, you'll run into a TV crew setting up a voyeuristic game show on it. But there are some travel tips that will help you enjoy some of the more exotic locales. For instance, when going through U.S. customs after a trip to Colombia with fifteen balloons of pure-grade Cackling Gecko Heroin in your stomach, always make sure to keep it light, okay? Smile at the customs agent's jokes but never giggle. *Never* giggle. And if one of the balloons should rupture and the dope starts to enter your bloodstream, try to cut short the cavity search by whispering over and over, "Oh yeah, daddy, that's the spot."

Speaking of lodging, hotels and I appear to differ on the precise definition of what constitutes a nonsmoking room. When I say "nonsmoking," I mean the room has only been occupied by people who don't smoke. Hotels' definition appears to be "Nobody's smoking in there right now." Two months ago, in New York, I stayed in a nonsmoking room that smelled like the guy before me had been curing a fucking ham.

Nowadays the big thing at hotels is to tell us that the energy used to clean and dry the bath towels is the number-one cause of global warming. Sorry, Sierra Club, but if it's a choice between the polar ice-caps melting and me using the same towel to dry my face that I use to dry my squatter, all I can say is "Surf's up, dude."

Some people like to travel by train because it combines the slowness of a car with the cramped public exposure of an airplane. But for most people, flying is the way to go. You know, airports have a curious smell that, I've finally deduced, is a delicate mixture of jet exhaust, bad food, spilled beer, and hundreds of thousands of armpits emitting numerous levels of toxicity according to various cultural hygienic mores. Try to picture an international rainbow of stink.

One of the more frustrating things about air travel is that you can't even relax when you land because you've still got that boot-camp obstacle course of baggage claim to negotiate. To all those people who insist on rushing to the carousel and staking out shoulder-to-shoulder body-wide territorial claims like it was the Yukon Gold Rush in 1890, will you jerkoffs just relax? Take a few steps back, Attila. No one is going to steal your duct-taped Styrofoam cooler full of pickled goat knuckles you brought back from the old country, all right? And to the elderly Eastern European women who think it's acceptable behavior to sever people's

Achilles tendons by ramming them from behind with those
rented baggage carts, let's try to keep the maiming to a minimum
or else that wall goes back up, okay, Olga?

Face it. The only reason we travel is so we can come back
and tell our tale of paradise, in order to lord it over other people. Like they give a shit. People only want to hear about your
trip if you had a miserable time, all right? They want horror stories because it validates their decision to stay home. You want to
make your friends happy? On your next vacation, pay too much
and lose a fucking eye.

Of course, that's just my opinion. I could be wrong.

MOB RULES

Can you believe the ratings for *Survivor*? Now, I don't want to get off on a rant here, but if HBO had aired new episodes of *The Sopranos* at the same time *Survivor* was on, do you really think anyone in America would have given a charbroiled rat's ass about who got voted out of that shitbox outback? Unlike most supposedly earth-shattering media events unleashed on us with the depressing regularity of Celine Dion farewell concerts, if there's anything that's lived up to its hype in the recent past, it is *The Sopranos*.

There's one thing I have to address before I continue. You might think that to devote an entire rant to another HBO program is corporate shilling of the most blatant sort. Nothing could be further from the truth. In fact, to even imagine that I could be reduced to the status of corporate mouthpiece is to impugn my integrity as a broadcaster, and I resent that accusation with the white-hot passion the San Francisco 49ers feel for the New England Patriots, *a game you dare not miss!*

I've been a big fan of *The Sopranos* from the beginning, but the growing impact it has had on television viewers across the board didn't really dawn on me until late one night when my mother-in-law called and asked me, and I quote, "Do you think Big Pussy has flipped?"

What draws us to stories about the mob? I think it's that unblinking mix of brutal, murderous savagery with the high premium placed on family loyalty, religion, and respect that people find so fascinating. A very low value placed on life by people who at the same time revere it. It's a complete contradiction, and where there's contradiction there's friction, and where there's friction there's heat, and where there's heat there's a story. Okay, class, that's all we have time for tonight, please read the chapter entitled "Say Hello to Mr. Subplot" in your signed copy of my book *It's the Story, Stupid!* and I'll see you here next week, and remember, two wrongs don't make a right, but a thousand wrongs make a writer . . .

To those who say that *The Sopranos* stereotypes all Italians as mooks and thugs, I say, turn off your politically correct radar and sit back and enjoy the show. Hey, it's filmed in North Jersey— if *The Sopranos* was really anti-Italian, that set would have more accidents than Halle Berry at a go-cart track.

I guess if I had one criticism of the show, it's why all the cursing? Maybe I'm old-school, but every time Tony Soprano says the f-word, it makes him come off like some kind of common hoodlum instead of the very prosperous and shrewd waste-management entrepreneur that he is. I love the dialogue on *The Sopranos*. You have the mundane day-to-day interactions of a hardworking suburban American family right up against literate little gems like "You know that blonde out there? I'd like to snap my dick off in that ass of hers." Where else on TV are you ever going to hear lines like that? Okay, maybe on *The Crocodile Hunter,* but no place else.

Tony Soprano is one of those characters I wish I could be more like. I'm almost there. I have a loving family and I'm often incapacitated by anxiety. I just have to work on that whole being-able-to-kick-someone's-ass thing. Tony Soprano is the perfect antihero. You realize he's a cold-blooded killer and an amoral criminal, but at the same time, he's a father trying to maintain the respect of his family. He knows he's a gangster, but he's trying to be the best gangster he can possibly be. And when you add it all up, at the end of the day it doesn't mean shit without money. Fuck logic. Fuck thoughtful analyses of great work. Just gimme the fuckin' money or, so help me God, I'll blow your motherfuckin' head off. Sorry. Woke up this morning and got myself a gun.

So, to David Chase and all the writers and directors, Tony, Carmela, Christopher, Janice, Richie, Potsie, Fonzi, Mr. C, Paulie, Dr. Melfi, Sylvio, AJ, Meadow, Adrianna, and everybody else—get ready, because to borrow a phrase from Uncle Junior, I got a feeling that at this year's Emmys you're gonna have the Television Academy so far up your ass you'll be tasting Brylcreem.

Of course, that's just my opinion. I could be wrong.

FREDDIE GETS THE FINGER

Now, I don't want to get off on a rant here, but the scariest thing about horror films nowadays is the freaks I have to stand in line with. Face it, horror movies have lost the subtlety and sense of ominous danger that once made them so compelling. How many times can you watch Jason Voorhees or Freddy Krueger or Michael Meyers or some other sworn enemy of clean-cut teenagers chew on the scenery like Lee Majors doing *Camelot* in summer stock? Hey, Jason, Freddy, Mike—you're omnipotent monsters, for chrissakes. Tone it down. Less is more. I've always thought that the monsters who talk about it the most, do it the least.

A good horror movie should have the right mix of eroticism and brutality, sex and violence, bush and gore. Horror and sex are as inseparable as Jekyll and Hyde. That's because horror films explore the dark side of human nature and, as we all know, sex is bad and dirty and people who have sex must be punished until they die. The movies that really scare me are not the ones set in a haunted house or outer space, but the ones that take place in the most familiar surroundings: a lonely street, a suburban home, a smoky waterfront bar filled with exotic men from many, many lands.

You know, horror is nothing new. During Elizabethan times, crowds flocked to the Globe Theatre to see Shakespeare's *Titus Andronicus,* an orgy of blood and vengeance. It was a big hit, although most agreed Shakespeare dropped the ball on his next one, *I Still Know What Titus Andronicus Did Last Mid-Summer.* My scariest movie moment came when I asked my lawyer if I could get out of *Bordello of Blood* and he said, "No, the contract is airtight."

One of the most popular horror gimmicks is taking an animal and making it much bigger than normal. That's how you get *Jaws* and *Cujo* and *King Kong.* My favorite has to be an obscure British film called *Big Freddy Wooten,* about a fifty-foot-tall, out-of-shape Anglican bishop who roams the landscape totally naked, bellowing, "It's the body God gave me!"

The first time I saw King Kong on top of the Empire State Building, I noticed something right away: no male gorilla genitalia. He's up there straddling the building, and there's no simian swingset hanging down. You go to any zoo and all the gorillas are packing serious nutsack. Kong? Nothing. Maybe that's why King Kong was really mad all the time. I know I'd be. Oh, maybe I wouldn't swat planes out of the sky, but I'd be very rude to waiters . . .

Of all the monsters, the Wolf Man had it the worst—more body hair than Ed Asner in a lint trap, never able to have a white couch in his house. Waking up after the full moon like he's coming off a bad meth jag, and hacking up fur balls for a week. Plus, what woman is going to understand when a guy tells her he's getting irrational because it's *his* time of the month?

The other day I was watching a Dracula movie starring Christopher Lee, who for my money was by far the most frightening vampire ever, and I found myself wishing that Lee really was a vampire just so I could take him backstage at a Marilyn Manson concert and watch that lightweight Goth wannabe shit his unitard.

Psycho is still the most disturbing film for me. The first time I saw it, the shower scene scared me so much that for the next two weeks I would only take *baths* in lonely motels run by creepy momma's boys. *The Exorcist* was a landmark movie: both scary and disturbing. It was also the first and last time a Catholic priest actually *wanted* to give a woman control over her own body.

The simple fact is, they don't make 'em like they used to. I blame *Scream,* which took the slasher/horror genre and turned it inside out. It was great for horror fans to follow along and be in on the joke the author was making about the horror movie, but that glimpse at the schematic shattered the mystery, like looking at the kitchen in a Chinese restaurant. *Scary Movie* poked fun of the movie that made fun of other scary movies. As a matter of fact, at this moment, I am writing a parody of the parody of the parody of scary movies called *Hey, Just Buy the Fucking Ticket!*

Of course, that's just my opinion. I could be wrong.

MAD AS HELL AND NOT GOING TO FAKE IT ANYMORE!

Now, I don't want to get off on a rant here, but our hair-trigger society has a fuse shorter than George W's attention span was at Yale. The latest rage that's all the rage is road rage. We use our middle finger so much, scientists say it may soon evolve its own brain.

I'll tell you what's scary—flipping off some asshole only to watch his car follow you all the way home and pull into the driveway behind you, causing you to cower on the floor of your car frantically dialing 911 until your wife comes out and explains that they're the friends that she invited over for dinner. The phenomenon of road rage, like many other curses on humanity, originated in Los Angeles, California, where you have to get in your car even if it's just to go get shot.

I have a simple solution for road rage: make everybody's license-plate number the same as their cell-phone number. That way, you can drive a safe distance away before you call the other car and tell them what assholes they are. Of course, that's assuming they have Asshole-Waiting.

The sickest and scariest kind of rage is the Hillary Clinton kind of rage. You know, the perpetual permafrost smile she wears that's hiding a full deep well, deeper than Barry White's voice during a bout of pneumonia.

America's a very uptight place now. Sure, we're making more money, but people are working longer hours, with some of us holding down two jobs in completely different fields at the same time . . . We're fighting more traffic, paying more for homes and food, and having to fuck around with more goddamn remote controls than ever. No wonder we've become touchier than a blind man reading *Penthouse Forum* in Braille.

Rage is not a completely unreasonable response to the stimuli around you nowadays. The meek may inherit the earth but, trust me, the assholes are going to contest the will. And occasionally you've gotta express your displeasure at the cosmic injustice of it all, but if a human being causes you extreme stress, the best thing to do is take it out on an inanimate object. Break a clock, kick in your TV set, or smash your computer screen with a ball-peen hammer. You'll feel a lot better. Just don't hurt anyone. Unless, of course, the cause of your rage is a malfunctioning piece of machinery. Then it's only fair to take it out on a human being, preferably somebody smaller than you. And, better yet, try digging up cemeteries and beating up people who are already dead. But considering this country's puritan attitude toward disinterment, it's best trying this one overseas. I guess what I'm advocating here is beating up foreign dead people. Sorta like a Hearafta-NAFTA.

During the past two decades we have become inundated with money and technology that allowed us to get accustomed to everything going our own way, which means we've got very little tolerance for frustration. The difference between the rage we see today and the rage of the '60s is this: road rage and air rage are the rage of the haves, not the have-nots. The people flying off the handle today are the people who have no reason to be upset about anything. Their rage is the by-product of an overfed, overindulged society of spineless, blathering crybabies. And it just makes me want to kick their fucking teeth in.

Of course, that's just my opinion. I could be wrong.

ME TALK
REAL GOOD

Midge. Moose. Moose. Midge. Alliteration is just one of the quirky little twists that one can use to augment the English language. English, for my jingoistic dollar, is still the crème de la crème of all languages. To listen to all the alarmist intellectual Henny-Penny doom-mongers going on and on these days about the imminent death of the English language, you'd think that the English language was, like, ya know, totally dying or something. Whatever.

Now, I don't want to get off on a rant here, but English is not just the language of Britain, Australia, Canada, and certain parts of Kentucky. It's also the language of business, diplomacy, and technology. I have always had a deep and abiding love for the

English language. I've always loved the flirtatious tango of consonants and vowels, the sturdy dependability of nouns and the capricious whimsy of verbs, the strutting pageantry of the adjective and the flitting evanescence of the adverb, all kept safe and orderly by those reliable little policemen, punctuation marks. Wow! Think I got my ass kicked much in high school?

You can gauge the esteem in which we hold the English language simply by telling someone you majored in it. The first thing they do is mentally subtract twenty grand off what they think you make for a living. The second thing they do is ask you to bring them a menu and tell them the soup of the day. And why not? In school, English was the easiest subject to bullshit your way through. There are no Cliff's Notes for Physics. You can't bluff your way through a Calculus discussion just by watching *Calculus: The Movie*. But when it comes to an essay question, you can fake it like a hooker being paid by-the-moan.

English is a protean, evolving language that must constantly change in order to remain relevant, but let's not go out of our way to appropriate words from other cultures simply to justify making something more expensive. You can add all the Italian suffixes you want, you're not fooling anybody over there at Starbucks—it's still just coffee. Now ring me the fuck up, you frappa-loser.

And Star*bucco*'s is not the only cultural borrower. Doctors tend to lift most of their phrases from Greek, which is only fitting since every time I go to see one, he somehow feels the need to spend the afternoon spelunking around in my ass.

I wouldn't be so worried about the fate of the English language if more of us could speak it properly. Forget Stone Cold Steve Austin or The Rock, if you want to see real wrestling, watch our president pronounce the word "unilateral." Love the guy or hate him, you have to admit that when Bush is speaking unscripted, the English language disintegrates like cotton candy in a monsoon. Even *he* looks like he's surprised at what's coming out of his mouth, kind of like John Malkovich when he had that puppeteer inside his head.

The English language is very much alive. From where I'm standing, our mother tongue is kicking ass and taking names. It's large and in charge. It's bright-eyed and bushy-tailed, full of piss and vinegar and ready to open up a big ol' can of whup-ass. It's calling the shots, it's bouncing and behaving, it's all up in it, and it's all that and a bag of chips. What the fuck am I talking about?

I have upon occasion been labeled the E. B. White of the word "fuck," but you have to admit that I went an entire football season without saying it. Take it from a connoisseur, it should be used sparingly, like saffron in a fucking paella. The word "fuck" is a beauty, isn't it? From its fricative genesis, blossoming into its ripe, rich middle until it's cruelly truncated in its prime by a merciless, glottal stop . . . In all of its earthy, salty illicit Anglo-Saxon glory, "fuck" is almost as satisfying to say as it is to do.

Some would say I contribute to the coarsening of the English language through my casual use of profanity. To those critics I

Show Business

HOLLYWOOD AND VAIN

Is there anybody who *doesn't* want to be on TV? Sometimes even on two different shows . . . in completely unrelated fields . . .

Now, I don't want to get off on a rant here, but while show business from the outside may seem like a nonstop whirlwind of gorgeous people, fabulous clothes, sparkling parties, and spectacular homes, the reality is . . . exactly that. Sorry, folks. I wish I had some balm to soothe you, but I don't. It's fucking awesome.

From Balinese shadow plays to bullfighters in Madrid to the porn studios of the San Fernando Valley to *The Craig Kilborn Show,* the only human desire more universal than the urge to put on a show is the urge to get paid for it. Show business is rife with paradox. It's brutally competitive and yet attracts people with egos as fragile as Strom Thurmond's hip. There's no doubt about it, show business lures the people who didn't get enough love early in life and have grown up to become bottomless, gaping vessels of terrifying, abject need . . . *Please* laugh NOW.

What draws the average person into a career in show business? Simple—they want to get laid. Take any of the Backstreet Boys or the kids from 'N Sync and put them behind a deli counter with a paper hat and day-old meat stains on their apron, and the only spears they'd have their hands on would be Vlasic Kosher Dills.

Sometimes I'll be flipping through the channels on my dish and I'll happen upon this television show from Iraq called *The Chabab Abeeely Program,* and this guy Chabab Abeeely looks really self-satisfied—singing, dancing, giving away the Chabab Abeeely home game to the Chabab Abeeely studio audience— and I always wonder: does Chabab Abeeely really think he, Chabab Abeeely, is in show business?

Why did *I* get into show business? For the same reason Chabab Abeeely did. In hopes of being immortalized by the no-frills Raymond-Chandler-if-he-had-no-talent narrative of the E! channel's smoke-enshrouded A. J. Benza. In the early '80s, I worked comedy clubs across the country nearly every week of the year. Many times I drove fifteen hundred miles at a time in a rusted-out AMC Pacer with tires balder than William Shatner fleeing his house during a three-A.M. earthquake, and a blinking dashboard warning-light sign that said "Hey, Asshole, Something's on Fire and It's Not Your Career" . . . All this just for the privilege of sharing a skanky one-bedroom apartment-slash-gulag with two other jerkoffs in skinny, crinkled ties, one of whom invariably had a cough so bad that a Welsh coal miner would tell him to get it checked out, and the other constantly bragged about getting laid by two different chicks every week for the past six years and screamed like Lawrence of Arabia galloping into Aqaba every time he tried to urinate.

Being in show business has its drawbacks . . . The other day I was at one of my favorite eateries and I got interrupted midbite by someone asking me, "Are you . . ." And I said, "Yes, I'm Dennis Miller. Can we do this later?" And he said, "Do what later? I wanted to know if you were finished with that ketchup?" The point I'm making is, if you're in show business, the only thing worse than getting interrupted for an autograph during a meal is *not* getting interrupted for an autograph during a meal. And when you begin to have more uninterrupted meals than Rudolf Hess in Spandau, it's time to consider another line of work.

Trust me, you don't want to overstay your welcome in this town. You start to panic, and everyone begins to see those rivulets of sweat running down your forehead, dripping off your chin, and it unnerves them, because they are then reminded of their own tenuous little toehold on the steep, shale cliffs of success, so they'll take any opportunity to loosen your pitons, causing you to plummet backward onto the jagged rocks at the base of the Piedmont and impale yourself on a stalagmite where the others still in the game can then watch the carrion birds feast on your exposed, still-warm entrails. Sing it with me: "There's no business like show business!"

In show business, it can take decades to become an overnight success, and only moments to be considered a lifetime failure. Ask Vanilla Ice. If he'll come out from under your car at Meineke. And don't think you can sleep your way to the top, because, I guarantee you, somebody's going to try to fuck you while you're sleeping. And the casting couch? A total myth! There is no couch. Trust me, it's never anything more comfortable than a rented card table covered in headshots . . . or so I've heard.

I would recommend this business only if you absolutely must receive constant attention to be happy and fulfilled and you have already proven yourself unqualified for a more pleasant profession, like being a medical test subject. Yes, the highs in show biz can be dazzling, but the views they provide are often straight to the bottom of the chasm ahead of you. I am sorry, young dreamer, but I cannot encourage you to join me in this difficult, wearying life, because I fear for your financial well-being, I am concerned about your mental health, I tremble at the pain you might cause yourself and your family, and, most important, I sure as shit don't need any more competition.

Bottom line: no matter how glamorous it appears to be, show business will always be a grueling and frequently humiliating industry. And you know what? I don't care whom you know, you never start out at the top, no matter what business you're in. First you're given oil wells, then you're given a baseball team, and then—and *only* then—are you given the White House.

Of course, that's just my opinion. I could be wrong.

Intolerance

TWELVE MILLION ANGRY MEN

Now, I don't want to get off on a rant here, but this country's so intolerant right now, they might as well change the plaque at the base of the Statue of Liberty to read GO THE FUCK BACK TO FUCKATANIA! I'll accept anyone's lifestyle, appearance, belief, or idiosyncrasy as long as they don't ask me to pay for it or wanna sit next to me on a plane and talk about it. What I object to are fringe groups who go beyond the notion of tolerance and demand our approval. Sorry, but if you move in next door to me, and one day I look out my window and see your wife cutting the lawn . . . with her teeth . . . because she's a fucking sheep, don't expect me to bring a covered dish over when you two reaffirm your vows, okay?

Intolerance leads people to do strange things: go to war, burn books, riot at soccer games, and eschew lactose, and there's never any logical reason for any of these actions. Most arguments made by intolerant people have all the consistency of space-shuttle Thanksgiving gravy. Why can't anyone just shut up and listen anymore? Whatever happened to the genteel art of sitting back and letting someone go on and on and on thinking he's right while you bask in the knowledge that he is completely full of shit?

Today's poster boy for intolerance is Eminem. I don't think there's really anything that damaging in Eminem's lyrics. He's no more dangerous than a bleached-blond Chihuahua chewin' on an old dishrag. Eminem doesn't upset me. You know why? Because he *wants* to upset me. Does his rap instill hate and inspire intolerance? All I can say is, not in me. As a matter of fact, it does the opposite. The more he talks about hating homosexuals, the more I urge gay inclusion in all aspects of society. The more crudely he rages against women, the more I crave their company and counsel. The more he casts blame on corporate responsibility for global warming resulting in the dangerous shrinking of the polar ice-caps, the more I realize that you now know that I'm totally full of shit and have never listened to his music.

The danger inherent in fighting intolerance is that often those attempting to eradicate it end up practicing it, only in a mutated, once-removed form. Liberals in particular are guilty of this supposedly well-meaning recidivism. It baffles me that the same people who blast away at President Bush's selection of a religious conservative for attorney general won't give George W. any kudos for his other cabinet choices, which include blacks,

Jews, Asians, Hispanics, and women. Does a fundamentalist Christian not also represent a valued strand in our collective fabric? Who's really being intolerant of other people's differences here? And, by the way, who cares if John Ashcroft's religion prohibits him from dancing? Who wants to see John Ashcroft dancing anyway? I hear he was born with two right feet.

And as for Senator Teddy Kennedy's quavering voice of righteous indignation constantly howling like a beagle at a Rick Wakeman concert at the prospect of a right-wing conservative holding sway over the country's law-enforcement priorities . . . Well, give it a rest, Spamhead. Let's not get into your view on women's rights and the sanctity of human life, because where those issues are concerned, Teddy, you may not be, uh, shall we say, in control of your own vehicle.

And let's not let conservatives off the hook. Especially the religious right. Quick show of hands: if he came down and applied, how many of you think Jesus would actually be accepted into Bob Jones University? C'mon, they'd beat the shit out of that long-haired, peace-and-love hippie before he could turn the first cheek.

You can never make everyone happy. The same people who scream about the freedom of choice for a woman to do what she wants with her body are forcing people who want *their* body to have a cigarette out into the streets to smoke. Some people who are against the death penalty are so adamant that they would electrocute those who are for it, and some of those who pray for the lives of the unborn also recite an extra "Our Father" when a clinic is bombed.

Tolerance does not mean you agree with everything other people say, or that you subordinate your best instincts to the tyranny of mass opinion. It simply means you pretend not to know that everyone on the planet but you is a fucking total moron. The most unforgivable thing about intolerance is that, by its inherent assumption that one group, belief, or lifestyle is superior to another, it fails to take into account the ultimate truth which binds us all, black and white, gay and straight, Republican and Democrat, Arab and Israeli, Hindu and Muslim, Catholic and Protestant, Serb and Croat, Hutu and Tutsi: the fact that, at the end of the day, we are all equal pains-in-the-ass in the eyes of the Lord.

Of course, that's just my opinion. I could be wrong.

Music Business

A SOUND DIVESTMENT

(FEB. 23, 2001)

See the Grammys this years? Christ, there were more subcategories than Larry Flynt's home-video library. I think somebody actually won for "Best Silence." Now, I don't want to get off on a rant here, but the music industry is in more trouble than a late-shift radar operator in Baghdad. Let's put our cards on the obsolete turntable: the music industry has nothing to do with music. What you hear on the radio today is one-half marketing, one-half public relations, and two-thirds timing. And if that math makes sense to you, you probably work in the royalties department at one of the major labels.

As I watched the Grammy Awards, I couldn't help but be struck by the fact that while our Founding Fathers guaranteed us all the right to freedom of speech, they never said anything about singing, okay? A lot of this stuff is just shit, and unwrapping the CD is often more complex than the thought that went into the music.

I love music. It gives you something to listen to while you're watching videos. And make no mistake, the music industry has turned itself into a visual medium and, that being the case, I feel I'm well within my rights to respectfully request that the members of Steely Dan never be allowed to appear on a prime-time telecast again. For chrissakes, for a second there, I thought I was watching *The X-Files*. Is it just me, or do the two guys in Steely Dan look like Ben & Jerry coming out of rehab? You know the only reason Steely Dan's latest album is selling so well is that fifty-year-olds don't know how to download it for free.

You know why Eminem showed up at the Grammys? Because it sells. Eminem isn't about freedom of speech as much as he is about the freedom to make a buck. He isn't peddling his songs underground to get his point across; he needs controversy to keep him famous because of his unfortunate dearth of talent.

Before you focus too much of your time and energy on loathing Eminem, let me spin this little scenario for you. Marilyn Manson watched the Grammys on a thirteen-inch black-and-white television set with a coat hanger for an antenna, at a Grange Hall in Bismark, North Dakota, after unveiling his apocalyptic vision for the future to fifty or so pasty-faced Goth losers who left during the encore so they could get home and watch *Temptation Island*. Trust me, Manson was so depressed that he is no longer in the crosshairs of the hate-rock controversy, that he could barely wriggle out of his fake vagina suit.

Pop music has a rich legacy of ripping people off. First the white musicians stole from the blacks. Then the producers stole from the performers. Then the performers and the producers formed an alliance to steal from *us* by charging nineteen dollars for a CD with only one halfway decent song on it. I for one salute Napster, because it's high time the public finally had an opportunity to horn in on a piece of the action. Considering how badly you get fucked every time you go into a record store, I have to assume Richard Branson was trying to be ironic when he named the place "Virgin."

Industry people will tell you that Napster is unfair and denies musicians their rightful, hard-earned cash. But musicians are going to waste their hard-earned cash anyway, okay?

They're *musicians*. Napster will only be a serious problem for the industry when it starts cutting into a musician's anonymous-pussy residuals.

The bottom line on Napster: it means no more paying for overpriced CDs and putting money into the pockets of the bloated, corrupt media conglomerates. All you need is a computer with a high-speed modem, extra memory, a CD-ROM attachment, an extra phone line, Internet access, a CD burner, blank CDs, a how-to manual, and *no fucking life*.

The music industry has always been about the coin. If they'd been invented at the time, Mozart would've sold T-shirts in the back of the hall. And Ticketmaestro would've skimmed their 20 percent off the top. While the sounds of U2 might be music to our ears, all the music industry hears is the soothing chime of the cash register. But the one thing you have to say about the music business is this: if the product is great, it will also be timeless. All you have to do is look at the *Billboard* charts to see that the Beatles are just as popular today as when Yoko broke them up. Not that I dwell on that . . . And, Yoko, by the way, if you're out there, why don't you level your karma and start dating one of the Baha Men.

Of course, that's just my opinion. I could be wrong.

The Clintons

IS HE GONE YET?

The Clintons left Washington about as quietly as Kid Rock leaves a Holiday Inn.

Now, I don't want to get off on a rant here, but like an infestation of cockroaches, a drunken party guest, or a super-virulent strain of antibiotic-resistant clap, the Clintons are proving almost impossible to get rid of. Is there any way for an entire nation to file a restraining order?

Since we first met them, Bill and Hillary's political relationship has been defined by a series of scandals, providing their marriage a much-needed distraction from ever having to actually stop and figure out how to extricate themselves from their biggest predicament: each other. Let's face it, if the Clintons' marriage were any more about convenience, they'd have to install a Slurpee machine and a Slim-Jim rack.

We all watched in astonishment as the Clintons moved out of the White House, merrily parading their greed and corruption past us like a garish Mardi Gras float powered by the drivetrain of Bill Clinton's gargantuan sense of entitlement. Hillary steers, while Bill sits on the top tossing pardons out to the crowd like a drunken Bacchus with a perpetual hard-on for a scepter.

It turns out, the Low Priest who shepherded many of the pardon petitioners to the quid-pro-quo altar was none other than Hillary's perpetually eight-and-a-half-months pregnant brother Hugh Rodham. Hey, who could blame Jabba the Hick for acting as a supersized go-between? How would you like it if your sister was in the White House for eight years and you couldn't even cash in on it because of stupid laws and shit? And the Hugh Rodham–sponsored pardons were small—and quickly eaten—potatoes compared to the Marc Rich debacle. Clinton has repeatedly insisted that his pardon of Marc Rich was the right thing to do. Which should probably tip you off to just how wrong it was. You almost have to admire the sheer audacity of granting pardons to two tax-scamming billionaire fugitives named "Rich" and "Green." If the symbolism were any more obvious, Andrew Lloyd Webber would be writing music for it.

And speaking of vacuous songwriters, the Marc Rich pardon was facilitated by his former wife, Denise Rich. Now, why would a former wife go to the wall for her ex-husband? Well, in this case, I can think of a couple of billion reasons. She couldn't be any more in her former husband's hip pocket if she were a piece of lint. Think about it. Denise Rich is the perfect foil to do the bidding of low-rent Machiavellis like her ex and Bill Clinton. Every time I see that footage of her standing there on stage next to Clinton in her strapless, fur-trimmed, hey-baby-give-it-up-you're-in-your-mid-fifties Escada frock, smiling that lobotomized, openmouthed smile, all the while clapping her mitts together like she's a trained seal cleaning erasers, just so thrilled to be part of the action that all the naysayers once told her was way out of her league, well, all I can think is, "Wow, she's not even aware of what an incredible dupe she's being played for." You know, there's nothing sadder than a starfucker who thinks she's a patriot. And I *like* her.

To be fair, it's not like other outgoing presidents and first ladies haven't been involved in sketchy pardons, taken gifts they weren't supposed to, or profited from their positions. It's just that no one has ever done it in such bulk, in so short a time, eliminating the midlevel operative and passing the scandal right on to you, the consumer. Let's face it: the Clintons are the Costco of sleaze. All of the lying, cheating, and stealing can't be good for either of the Clintons' karma. At this point, Hillary's coming back as a dung beetle with an overdeveloped sense of smell and Bill will come back as . . . uh . . . probably Bill. This guy's smarter than God. Never count Bill Clinton out. When the whole world has turned its back on him, when the baying hounds are confusing the scent of *his* blood with somebody else's who's about to take the fall for him . . . That is the precise moment he has you exactly where he wants you.

Perhaps Bill Clinton didn't so much betray his allies as seduce them into betraying themselves. From the women's-rights groups who took Clinton's side against all the women he victimized to all the liberal compadres he discarded when it was politically expedient to do so, Clinton's proffered deal has always been the same: I will help you achieve your goals if you simply abandon the ideals that made them worthwhile in the first place.

I guess what I'm saying, Bill, is "We're on to you and it's over, understand?" We've awakened from our long nightmare of codependence and addiction and we've found someone new. Maybe he's not as smart or as exciting as you, but he treats us nice and makes us feel pretty. We don't need you anymore, Bill, okay? So, stop calling and stop driving past our house at night and stop looking at us like that. Now get off the porch and get out of here . . . before we change our minds.

Of course, that's just my opinion. I could be wrong.

Shrinks

PSYCHIATRIC COUCH POTATOES

An article in *USA Today* this week reported an increase in the number of pet owners taking their dogs to see psychiatrists. Whatever happened to yelling at your dog to get *off* the couch? You know, if I could lick my own balls, I sure as hell wouldn't need a shrink. Ah, whom am I kidding? I *can* lick my own balls. That's why I go to a shrink. I can't stop. Because I'm a human being, with a bafflingly complex mind . . . and a very stiff neck.

Now, I don't want to get off on a rant here, but even the best psychiatrist is like a blindfolded auto mechanic poking around under your hood with a giant foam WE'RE #1 finger. Though definitely a Western phenomenon, psychiatry harkens back to traditional, tribal forms of healing, in which the right combination of words and potions would ease your tortured spirit. I can just picture an African Bushman, lying on a dirt floor, anxiously telling his medicine man this nightmare he keeps having about showing up at work fully clothed.

Even though it was invented in Europe, only here in the United States could psychiatry become the multimillion-dollar business it is today. We're the only people in the world who are stupid enough to actually want to know what's going on inside our minds. Americans couldn't be any more self-absorbed if they were made of equal parts water and paper towel.

Another reason psychiatry has flourished in the United States is that in the '70s, Woody Allen helped popularize the idea that going to a shrink is normal and healthy. Just look what it's done for him and his family. You know, he and his daughter-slash-wife have never been happier.

Since the days of Freud, psychiatry has been strictly limited to the realm of the middle and upper classes. Psychoanalysis is expensive, which isn't too surprising when you consider it was invented by a major cokehead. The difference between psychiatry and psychology is just one of those little nagging things I can never remember. Like stalactite or stalagmite. Alligator or crocodile. Nipple clamp or nipple restraint. Sweet pleasure or sweet, sweet pleasure . . .

Rather than dwelling on childhood traumas and repressed sexuality, modern psychiatry deals more with correcting chemical imbalances in the brain. Kind of like what some people did back in college, except then it wasn't called psychiatry, it was called "bong hits." Therapists face the daunting task of taking chaotic, violent, and unstable people and molding them into well-rounded, secure, and productive members . . . of a chaotic, violent, and unstable society.

I'm not saying we should return to the days of lobotomies and electroshock, but I do feel the pendulum has swung way too far the other way. Today, everything is a disorder or a disease that deserves our understanding. Nobody is held responsible for any of their actions, and that's gotta go. I think a good first step would be to change "not guilty by reason of insanity" to "guilty by reason of insanity."

I'm a pretty normal guy when it comes to my mental health. If I have one little problem that sometimes makes me consider seeing a shrink, it's a white-hot hatred for all humanity that burns so intensely it literally sears my insides. Other than that, I'm feelin' pretty mellow these days. All kidding aside, I know what my problem is. I'm what you'd call a self-loathing paranoid. I don't think I'm worth the time and effort it would take for someone to hunt me down.

I view my head in much the same way I view the television set. When something isn't working right, I can either bang it with my hand or call on a professional to fix the damn thing. In fact, I even have my shrink wear a tool belt and a name tag, and rip a big one at the start of every session. The key is to find a therapist that you click with—someone you trust implicitly with the deep, dark secrets that you wouldn't even tell your accountant. I've had some great therapists and I've also had some who left me questioning their credentials. The worst was Doctor Cletus, a Jungian in bib overalls who, while I poured out the most intimate details of my very existence, would thumb through back issues of *Guns & Ammo,* occasionally glancing over at me, giggling, and muttering, "Man, that is some weird-ass shit."

The best input I ever got from a shrink? When I was younger, I was plagued by feelings of inadequacy. So I went to see a psychologist, and he told me the reason I felt inadequate was because I *was* inadequate. *That* guy was a fucking genius.

Of course, that's just my opinion. I could be wrong.

BET YOU CAN'T BORROW JUST ONE

Now, I don't want to get off on a rant here, but why are Americans so in love with credit? Simple: *we're Americans*. We want everything, we want it bigger, louder, shinier, faster, and we want it *now*. Instant gratification is as American as drive-through microwave apple pie. *Of course* Tantric sex was invented in India. Here, we want to fuck just to get it over with so we can go out and buy more shit.

This country was founded on debt. Right off the bat, we got ourselves into hock to pay for the Revolutionary War. In 1803, we purchased the Louisiana Territory, and they only sent us the clear title for that three weeks ago.

You can't begin to understand credit until you understand its boozy counterpart, interest. Credit is like a friendly bartender, wrapping his arm around your shoulder and telling you it's okay, just put this round on your credit card and take care of it with your next paycheck. Interest is the surly bouncer who hustles you head-first out of the warm tavern and face-first into the urine-stained snowbank, all the while mercilessly punching you in the ribs as he methodically goes through your pockets until he gets back every last penny that you owe him.

Even the thriftiest among us need credit at some point. When you mortgage a house. When you buy a car. When you're on eBay and you see a mint-condition ice-packed human kidney that's still throbbing and would go perfectly in your collection. But who would have a collection like that . . . Clarice?

The irony is that responsible people who pay as they go never build up a good credit rating. And without one, you're considered a bad lending risk. Just try applying for a car loan or a mortgage. Trust me, you'll be ignored like the busboy at Hooters.

There is a whole generation out there that, between ATM cards and credit cards, doesn't even know what cash looks like. You take out a wad of bills these days to pay for that pizza and you might as well be pulling out beaver pelts. I have had cashiers take the twenty-dollar bill I've given them and write my driver's license number on it. Of course, we'll always need cash for strip clubs. Nobody wants to see a naked chick swipe a card.

I know what it's like to have bad credit. When I was nineteen, credit card companies would send me letters telling me I had been preapproved for rejection. Giving teenagers a credit card to teach them about money is like getting them drunk and putting them behind the wheel of a car to teach them responsibility. The interest rates on these cards make Tony Soprano look like George Bailey.

Bottom line: this country is more dependent on plastic than the casting director for Pamela Anderson's *V.I.P.* And while I appreciate the convenience credit cards provide, what I really like are the cards themselves. I like their size and weight—as a matter of fact, I have customized mine with razor-sharp tungsten edges and balanced them for throwing with deadly accuracy. I also took the liberty of having a graphic artist rework the little holograms on the cards. My MasterCard shows a squirrel water-skiing, and my Visa shows an old, fat couple fucking.

If I have one bone to pick with the credit card companies, it's that they make the place where you're supposed to put your signature on the back of the card too small. And nobody ever checks the signature on the card anyway. When they do, it's just for show; they're not really checking it. I know, because on my most recent card, instead of signing it, I wrote "Just ring it up, shithead." And, so far, not a peep.

One of the ways we judge which rung of the ladder you are perched on in this society is by what color credit card you carry. For American Express, the once-prestigious Green card can be replaced by the Gold card. Keep charging, and you are eligible for the Platinum card, which can now be trumped by the upper-echelon Black card. Soon you will be able to just have a bar code sewn onto your ass, and then there will be *absolutely no way* you can leave home without it.

I am fortunate, because I have the money to pay off my credit cards at the end of each month—but I choose not to. Why? Well, if a killer asteroid obliterates the earth, causing tidal waves and cosmic fires that destroy every submicroscopic trace of life on this planet as we know it, and I still owe three grand on my Visa, I win.

Of course, that's just my opinion. I could be wrong.

Hipsters

GOOD-BYE, COOL, COOL WORLD

You know why Jack Kerouac was cool? Because he had no idea he was. Now, I don't want to get off on a rant here, but cool is a gift. It's having eight pounds of hip in a five-pound bucket. It's not bought, bred, or bequeathed. Clinton lost it, Gore can't buy it, and Bush thinks it's spelled with a *K*.

America's drive to be cool is like an endless game of "Follow the Leader," with all of us in a dogsled train, struggling to keep up with the alpha-male trendsetter, when all we can make out are the hazy, glistening outlines of his ice-flecked, rhythmically pumping butt cheeks . . . Sorry, I got a little carried away there. I'm still recovering from Gay Week on Animal Planet.

The United States is the birthplace of cool. If the world was a high school, America would be making out in study hall with Sweden, picking on India, and smoking in the U.N. restroom with France.

There are many types of cool. There's the classic, iconic, Bogart approach: cryptic and unflappable, squinting through the smoke from the cigarette dangling between your lips, never letting a trace of emotion show except for an occasional sardonic half-smile at the foolish world around you that you couldn't give a rat's ass about. Some celebrities reach a cool of such mythic proportion that it transcends their physical being. Sinatra was so cool, he hadn't bothered to take a breath for years even when he was alive, and he could still kick the shit out of you.

Then there's the demographically researched, pop-media faux cool, the type of insouciance that bears the corporate patina of mass-marketed nonconformity. This is shopping-mall cool, easily attainable—you don't have to Harley to Sturges, or master the guitar, or trek through Nepal; just plunk down your Discover card and buy some threads at Urban Outfitters or a barbed-wire bicep-tattoo at the Henna Hut, and not only will you enter the kingdom of cool, you'll also get a valuable cash-back bonus that can be applied to cruise travel or a *Reader's Digest* subscription.

I think some manufacturers may be trying a little too hard to envelop everything with a hip aura. I was at the drugstore and watched an old man spend fifteen minutes trying to decide if he wanted his Ex-Lax in Extreme Orange or Totally Wacked

Wintermint. There are certain places and situations where it's virtually impossible to put up a cool front. For example, when your doctor gives you a prostate exam, or when the supermarket cashier calls for a price check on supersmall-sized condoms, or when the doorman at the *Vanity Fair* Oscar party bitch-slaps you for bursting into tears when he tells you he can't find your name on the guest list.

I guess the coolest I ever felt was when Dana Carvey's Church Lady was really taking off on *Saturday Night Live,* and yet the entire nation was doing *my* George Bush impersonation. Oh, wait, that was Dana, too. Come to think of it, I've never felt cool. One of my favorite pastimes is to try to determine who the coolest person in the room is. The other day at Starbucks, as I observed the twentysomething counter jockey with the pierced prefrontal cortex and the dust bunny on his chin, and the as-yet-unproduced screenwriter sitting in the corner staring at a four-year-old script-in-progress that still had fewer words in it than his latte order, and the heavily perfumed walking designer rack talking into her cell phone like she was trying to be heard over a fucking chain saw, I realized with some pride that I was the coolest person in the immediate proximity . . . until I looked out the window and caught the eye of the Guatemalan landscaper trimming the hedges, obviously wondering what kind of schmuck I was to pay three dollars and seventy-five cents for a cup of coffee.

Bottom line: the only real cool people left are those who don't buy into the coolness mystique. People who don't take themselves too seriously, and don't screw over other people, and

DON'T TRY THIS AT HOME . . . WE REALLY MEAN IT THIS TIME

This weekend, ESPN is holding its first Extreme Sports awards. "Extreme sports"? Folks, let's call this what it is: weird shit invented by guys who are willing to die to get laid. Now, I don't want to get off on a rant here, but our obsession with extreme sports has people all over the country jumping off bridges, skyscrapers, and mountain cliffs, and some of them aren't even invested in the stock market.

The concept of extreme sports is yet another component in the vast conspiracy contrived to make me feel like I'm aging faster than a tuna sandwich in the glove compartment of a black car parked in Phoenix, Arizona. Extreme sports are usually played by middle-class white kids because, quite frankly, the equipment involved is expensive, the activities often require costly trips to exotic locations, and, let's face it, if you're growing up in an inner-city housing project, the mere act of walking to school is, no doubt, extreme enough for you.

Gen-X sports have been so successful for advertisers that they're now afraid to market anything without them. I saw Charles Schwab on TV the other day, trying to yell something about moderate-growth mutual funds while wakeboarding off the North Shore of Oahu, with his knee joints poppin' like two M-80s goin' off in an underground parking garage. You only have to watch a minute of extreme sports to distill what is really going on here: psychopaths enriching osteopaths.

When it was first introduced, bungee jumping was the peak of extreme, a wild, daring pastime only the boldest madmen would undertake. Today it has become so mainstream that all bungee-jumping platforms are required by law to be fully wheelchair-accessible. Then there's BASE jumping, a high-fatality activity that involves leaping off buildings and bridges with a parachute. When I was ten years old, I climbed up on the roof of our neighbor's garage and jumped off while holding an open umbrella. Only it wasn't called BASE jumping back then . . . let's see, what was it called . . . oh yeah, "Being a fucking *moron*." If you really want to screw with a BASE jumper's head, wait at the edge of the cliff and, just before he's about to go, ask for his girlfriend's phone number.

When I watch one of these eco-challenge events, I always wonder what the local natives think when they see the civilized folk "roughing it" with all the state-of-the-art clothing and equipment money can buy. Meanwhile, the Sherpas are climbing Everest with nothing on their feet but Wonder Bread bags. And how about when these hikers pull out their calorically calibrated protein bars while the guide from the tribe, naked except for the animal horn on his penis, just digs into a pile of elephant dung, pulls out an undigested peanut, and calls it macaroni?

Extreme sports are fascinating to someone like me, who screams like Maria Callas in late-stage labor if I drive over a pothole with an open coffee container between my legs. I also think I speak for many of my fellow Los Angelenos when I say that I find extreme sports redundant when I spend a good deal of my day just trying to stay alive in traffic while pinned between four stegosaurus-sized SUVs, each being driven by a psychotically aggressive, Palm Pilot–wielding, ninety-eight-pound woman with the blood-sugar level of Lot's wife.

I view *professional* extreme athletes with, at worst, mild puzzlement and, at best, genuine respect. But what pisses me off are the *amateur* extreme athletes, who don't just risk their own lives—they make some park ranger, fireman, or cop risk *his* life to save them. Every time I see a soldier who enlisted so he could defend his country having to put his neck on the line, rappelling off a helicopter to save some middle-aged hero-wannabe jagoff who skied twenty miles off the clearly marked trail just so he can have a better pickup line than "Hey, baby, your place or my mom's?," I can't help but hope that just this one time, the kid from the National Guard is going to change his mind and chopper away to get a well-deserved beer, but not before getting close enough to shout: "Hey, asshole, Charles Darwin says hi."

Of course, that's just my opinion. I could be wrong.

UP NEXT: YOUR COLONOSCOPY ON *20/20!*

Madonna is shameless about publicity, isn't she? I find it hard to sympathize too much when she calls a live, televised, webcast, stereo-simulcast, distributed-by-satellite, available-on-properly-equipped-cell-phones press conference to complain that the media doesn't respect her privacy. The only time Madonna *doesn't* draw a crowd is the opening weekend of one of her films. Now, I don't want to get off on a rant here, but why is it that the only people who are quiet and mind their own business nowadays are the serial killers? Americans stick their nose where it doesn't belong more than Cyrano de Bergerac giving head. We live in a nauseatingly confessional society, but it wasn't always that way.

There was a time when you wouldn't dream of telling a guy you just met that you were an alcoholic. Unless, of course, you met the guy because you had driven your car into his swimming pool.

Thanks to our tight-lipped Puritan ancestors with their scarlet letters and witch-hunts, we've always been a nation obsessed with the doings of others. In the past, however, we justified our meddling with some lame, moralistic claptrap about "upholding community standards." Well, community standards have now deteriorated like the relationship between Brett Michaels and C. C. Deville on VH1's *Poison: Behind the Music*. And, by the way, I hear Poison is touring again. It's always nice to go see a retro-tour of a hair band where the only drug they're now shooting up is Rogaine.

The thing about the entertainment media's brand of voyeurism is, we're so easily bored that if somebody wants to keep our attention, they must continually supersize the freak value. I was watching *Springer* the other day and saw a couple get their marriage back on track by beating the shit out of each other. I think Jerry's final thought was entitled, "I'm OK, You're OK, Bitch."

Then there are the hapless casualties of voyeurism, like Monica, Darva, and Kato, forced to watch defenselessly as every nook and cranny of their personal lives gets slurped into America's bottomless maw for other people's humiliation—all under the false rubric that a free and open society has the right to know. At first fidgety, these quasi-luminaries ease into their new roles quickly, seduced by the yodeling highs of celebrity that smudge the line between the famous and the infamous, until there's no real point in their ever saying good-bye, is there? They turn into Abe Vigoda—you always think they're dead, and yet they're always RSVP'ing in the affirmative. It's sort of like karmic extortion. We wouldn't leave them alone, so now it's their turn.

What I can't fathom are the people who auction off their privacy on the open market. You can go on-line now and watch mutants and cybergeeks who record every nanosecond of their lives—every snore, every burp, every restraining order filed against them by William Shatner—and then beam it out over the Internet. It all raises the interesting philosophical question: how can you broadcast your life when you don't have a life?

Do the media and the Internet feed this tendency or merely reflect it? We're living in a time when personal boundaries are more blurred than the camera lens in a Joan Collins photo shoot. You would think that this would help to generate more openness between people, but all it seems to have done is increase our mistrust. We feel perfectly comfortable spending hours on-line, sharing our innermost thoughts and yearnings with strangers, but we don't even meet the people living next door to us until there's a huge earthquake and everyone's out on their lawns at one in the morning. As a matter of fact, that's the scariest part of an earthquake—hearing your fifty-eight-year-old neighbors Myrna and Leo explain how they had just strapped her into the Vietnamese fuck basket when, all of a sudden, she started swinging back and forth, like King Kong's balls on a hot day. "Well, thanks for the visual, Myrna, I think I'm gonna go pick up a downed power line now, okay?"

One of the most disturbing trends in the demise of personal privacy is the proliferation of hidden cameras. I just don't think that's right. When I'm by myself, just like everyone else in this room, I do things that I would never do if I knew I was being videotaped. I pick my nose. I scratch my nuts. I squeeze blemishes. I work at my stubborn dandruff patch. I kick off my shoes and bite my toenails. I use whatever's lying around to scrape my tongue. I pull nostril hairs out and measure them with a small silver ruler I carry on a chain around my neck and record their length in millimeters in an embossed spiral notebook. I pinch my nipples until my eyes tear up, and I straddle things and yell "giddy-up" while slapping myself on the ass with a Victorian carpet beater. The point is, I should be able to pass my time waiting in line at the post office any way I want to.

Of course, that's just my opinion. I could be wrong.

TIPS FOR INVESTING IN A BULLSHIT MARKET

Lately, the stock market's been performing like a blind dominatrix—you never know when she's going to hit bottom. Now, I don't want to get off on a rant here, but the stock market is Las Vegas without the slots, the hookers, or the dependable odds.

Two phrases you'll often hear are "bull market" and "bear market." A bear market is where I lose money because my stocks are plummeting along with everybody else's, while a bull market is where I lose money because my stocks are plummeting all by themselves.

Analysts are always telling us that the best way to invest in stocks is for the long term. The only problem is that in an attention-deficit-disordered America, "long term" indicates a time unit somewhere between the career of a boy band and the bitch-slap of a hummingbird. And now, with the advent of the Internet, an unholy alliance between the home computer and the stock market has spawned the day trader—the kind of proto-loser who is spot-welded into his Incredible Hulk underoos down in the basement, his trembling, silver-Lotto-scratch-card-dust-encrusted fingernails frantically pounding "buy" and "sell" orders into his keyboard so loudly that he can't hear his mother upstairs crying out for the good old days when all he did on-line was compulsively masturbate.

The widely held gospel of Wall Street is "buy low and sell high." Thanks for the tip. That's like telling a bald guy, "Getting laid's easy—just go to a bar and pick up Heidi Klum." When the market began to tank last month, I couldn't get my broker on the phone. Finally, his secretary admitted that he had quit to take a job with Exxon, but she couldn't remember which gas station it was.

I've learned some painful lessons about investing. In the future, when ending conversations with an investment advisor, I will say, "I'm done speaking with you now," instead of "bye-bye," which my former money manager always mistook for an enthusiastic request to purchase shares in whatever lean-to piece-of-shit-dot-com sham he was getting blow jobs and free plane tickets to push that week.

There's no substitute for doing your homework before investing in a company—good, solid, fiscal research. When I'm thinking of investing in a retail chain, for example, I go to one of their stores and lock myself in a bathroom stall. Then I curl up in a fetal ball on the floor and emit a low, painful-sounding groan, and time how long it takes one of the assistant managers to come in and see if I'm okay. Wal-Mart? Three minutes. Target? Half hour. Kmart? Kibbel the night janitor woke me up at three in the morning and asked if I had any rolling papers.

I know investing is a risky proposition, and I don't mind losing my shirt, but can I have my pants back? Recently, I put sixty thousand dollars into Krispy Kreme doughnuts. Thank God, I didn't buy any stock. Last year I bought Pets.com at thirty. Two weeks later, it was dropping faster than Al Roker on a greasy flagpole. You'd think I would have learned my lesson, but I moved my remaining liquid capital into something called eToys. Last time I looked, their stock had broken through zero and was tunneling into the molten magma at the core of our planet.

The gloomy end of the unsurpassed bull market of the '90s did turn up some unexpected bright spots. For one thing, remember that day-trading dilettante prick neighbor of yours—the guy who threw a few lucky darts at the NASDAQ wheel and showed up at every party for the next year in his Lincoln Navigator, downed a few too many glasses of Turning Leaf Chardonnay, and got all self-important, going on and on like he was Warren Buffett with a soul-patch talking about P/E ratios and small-cap funds' place in the Keynesean oeuvre and you figured, "Well, he must know what he's talking about," and so you put ten grand in a stock he recommended that collapsed like the Three Stooges' tent the following week? You remember that guy? Well, right about now he's replacing all the deodorant cakes in the men's-room urinals at Der Wienerschnitzel before he finishes off his shift standing out front and handing out half-off chili fry coupons, dressed like a giant fuckin' bratwurst. I'd say karma is up about a hundred points.

Of course, that's just my opinion. I could be wrong.

SURVIVING *SURVIVOR*

Now, I don't want to get off on a rant here, but what does it say about our culture when the most escapist form of entertainment is called "reality television"? In the past, most networks dabbled delicately in the arena of reality TV, but lately, they've been going for it like a hungry mutt for an ass-flavored Milk-Bone. One of the longest-running reality shows is *Cops,* every episode of which poses the burning question: why is that morbidly obese man not wearing a shirt? At least digitally scramble his man-tits, okay?

Then there's *The Real World,* based on the premise that living rent-free in a fabulous house on the beach with a bunch of attractive young people while being videotaped by an ever-present camera crew is in any way, shape, or form, real. However, *The*

Real World does provide us with the valuable insight that, like, when you buy, like, orange juice, you know, and somebody else, like, drinks it without, you know, like, asking, that's, like, a personal violation? You know?

I couldn't watch *Temptation Island,* because it would have reminded me of one of my vacations when I was single. Remember when you planned to hit the island and fuck anything that moved . . . and nothing moved?

Survivor is the gold standard of reality programming. If I were a contestant on *Survivor,* I would probably be one of the first to be voted off—if not for my tendency to openly hate other people, then for the visual and emotional assault that is I in bicycle pants, crying all the time. My plan would be simple. As soon as the votes were tallied and Jeff Probst gave me the bad news, saying, "The tribe has spoken," I'd say, "Oh yeah? Well, fuck the tribe. I'm a 'Survivor'!" and I'd bolt into the jungle, only to emerge every night to pick the other contestants off one by one with poison darts. Then I'd start in on the crew.

Now they've started double-layering the reality shows. They've had everything from *Dateline* stories on *Big Brother* to the *Survivor* cast on *The Weakest Link.* I'm not sure they've taken it far enough. I wouldn't mind seeing that frigid dwarf chick from *The Weakest Link,* caught in nothing but her chainmail corset and size-2 jackboots, running down an alley, being chased by an immigration officer, on a Fox special called *When Untalented Foreigners Get Hired.*

But while I've got bones to pick with it, I do think reality television has a place in the roster of our nightly entertainment. In fact, I have several ideas for new shows. The first is called *You Gotta Be Shittin' Me*—it involves simply mounting video cameras atop gasoline pumps at stations throughout Southern California. I'm also pitching an alternative to *When Good Pets Go Bad* called *Put the Goddamn Video Camera Down, Edna, and Yank This Mongoose Off My Nutsack.*

The key thing to remember about this evolutionary stage in the medium is that TV tends to eat its own. In a classic example of plagiaristic television logic, the geniuses at NBC noticed that every successful reality show sparked its own catchphrase— "Voted Off the Island," "Is That Your Final Answer?"—so they decided that all they needed to make a hit out of *The Weakest Link* was to plaster the phrase "You Are the Weakest Link" over so many billboards and bus stops that it is now permanently burned into my brain like that time I walked in on Star Jones in the VIP bathroom. But you know what? You cannot build an entire show around a single, easily remembered catchphrase, and assume that just because you repeat it week after week, people will ultimately attach some sort of profundity or wit to it and clap like trained seals whenever they hear it. People are not that stupid. They're not going to fall for it.

Of course, that's just my opinion. I could be wrong.

WHERE THERE'S SMOKE, THERE'S PROFIT

Now, I don't want to get off on a rant here, but tobacco is so entwined with the history of this country that the only reason the Statue of Liberty is not holding up a lit cigarette is that her torch provides a better backdrop for final showdowns in shitty action movies.

If you ask most smokers whether they want to smoke, they'll probably tell you no, they hate it, but nicotine couldn't be tougher to kick if Lucy Van Pelt from *Peanuts* was holding it with her fingertips. Los Angelenos have been some of the most outspoken advocates against smokers exposing us to their sec-

ondhand smoke. Which is ironic, considering that compared to
L.A. air, secondhand smoke is like aromatherapy. The L.A.
basin—God's ashtray.

As everyone who saw *The Insider* will remember, Russell
Crowe's character, in trying to testify against the tobacco industry, was up against an adversary that would do anything to stop
him, from e-mailing him threats to targeting his wife and child
to forcing him to fight off man-eating lions on the blood-
drenched floor of the Colosseum.

By definition, the tobacco companies' best customers are the
ones most likely to up and die on them, so they must constantly
look for fresh meat. As a result, they aim their laser sites on the
group of people who are easy prey because they are so naive, so
easily swayed by peer pressure, and so unprepared to make their
own decisions as mature adults: Southerners. Also, teenagers.
They start 'em off young. Remember candy cigarettes? I used to
love those. At first, I only enjoyed one with an occasional glass
of Kool-Aid or, say, after a wild and crazy Slip-and-Slide party at
Ray Luigi's place, but pretty soon I was up to three packs a day.
I never went in for bubblegum cigars, though; they always
seemed a tad pretentious.

Our war on tobacco is a microcosm of a fundamental contradiction in the American psyche. We see ourselves as independent,
livin'-my-life-without-the-government-on-my-back Marlboro men
until something goes wrong, whereupon we turn into whiny, liti-
gious crybabies looking for someone to foot the bill for our
fuck-ups. There's a raft of ex-smokers suing tobacco companies
because they got sick, and I don't think that's right. Sure, I *hate*

tobacco companies and think they sell a quintessentially evil product, and then lie through their yellowed teeth, all the while trading in their venal, profiteering souls for a lucrative paycheck, knowing full well they'll have their flesh raked by the fiery claws of Hell, while the cries of all their victims resonate in their ears, for all eternity. That being said, I hate lawyers even more.

I feel sorry for the people suffering the effects of years of smoking. Yes, I think the tobacco companies should be punished for their deceptions and subterfuge. But suing a tobacco company because you've developed a health problem from smoking cigarettes is like suing McDonald's because they failed to inform you that hot coffee will scald your lap if you spill it on yourself. Okay, bad example. Try this one: suing a tobacco company because you've developed a health problem from smoking cigarettes is like demanding an apology from the Members Only–jacket people for your not getting laid in the 1980s.

The tobacco companies are missing out on a massive PR opportunity to turn the tide of public opinion in their favor. I'm speaking, of course, about the energy crisis and the surrounding environmental concerns. If the lights go out during an unexpected rolling blackout, who's going to have a lighter to provide emergency illumination? The smoker. If we experience increased pollution from unregulated power plants, who's going to require less oxygen because of diminished lung capacity? The smoker. And if ecosystems fall like dominoes, rendering the human race a band of cannibalistic scavengers wandering through a barren wasteland, whose flesh will possess the pleasant smoky taste of barbecue? The smoker's.

America grows most of the world's tobacco. If I were president, I'd go on television and tell those jagoffs from OPEC, "Hey, you know what's tougher to kick than cheap oil? Those Yankee Devil Marlboro 100s that you're always lightin' up off a burning American flag. Yeah, that's right, Sheik Octane, you heard me. I don't see any tobacco plants sprouting up from that desert shitbox of yours, all right? Now I want to see premium gasoline going for fifty cents a gallon again, or you guys are going to be up all night chain-sucking on goat-flavored Jolly Ranchers."

Of course, that's just my opinion. I could be wrong.

LIFE IS A PITCH

Remember Saturday-morning cartoons? Two minutes of filler between commercials for supersoakers and sixteen thousand forms of sugar, including salted sugar. Now, I don't want to get off on a rant here, but I think advertising is necessary, because it often imparts vital information to the consumer. For example, paper towels with two plies are more absorbent. Wider gaps in tire treads help prevent hydroplaning. Fluoride fights tooth decay. Visiting foreign countries makes you shit yourself. And then you're back to the two-ply thing. It's the circle of life.

Advertising is not merely a human phenomenon but a biological impulse found throughout the natural world. Peacocks attract mates through a multicolored feather display. Baboons signal their sexual readiness with a pair of red, swollen buttocks. And both the duck and gecko offer a broad range of attractively priced car-insurance packages.

TV commercials nowadays are unrecognizable from what they were twenty years ago. Now you get these out-of-focus MTV jump-cuts with a throbbing techno soundtrack, writhing supermodels in tankinis simulating lesbian sex in the rain, a nun riding a yellow bike, and a little barefoot kid in a Guatemalan village—and it's an ad for fucking pretzels.

I wish the people who wrote those catchy commercial jingles in the '70s had taught at my high school—I think I would've retained a lot more useful knowledge. I don't remember anything about geometry, but I do remember that when it says Libby's, Libby's, Libby's on the label, label, label, you will like it, like it, like it on your table, table, table. (Thank you, thank you, thank you.) If I find myself alone in my car one more time singing, "Plop-plop, fizz-fizz, oh what a relief it is," I'm going to hunt down the mind-control fuckwad who wrote that piece-of-shit Pavlovian haiku and demand he give me back that part of my brain.

I'm seeing a lot more ads for medicines now. They're pushing pills for allergies with a list of side effects that reads like a book of witch's spells. Nosebleeds, dry mouth, insomnia, shortness of breath, liver damage. You know what? Keep your allergy medicine, okay? I'd rather reach for a Kleenex than have a blue arc of electricity connecting my nipples.

At the top of my list of commercials I like are the ones for the local stereo store starring either the stereo-store owner, or the heavily made-up stereo-store receptionist that the stereo-store owner is trying to bang. I'm all for sex in advertising, but I think it has gone too far. Steamy, provocative magazine ads are fine, but I was at the beach recently, and there was a prop plane going back and forth along the shoreline trailing a banner that said: ADD INCHES TO YOUR TINY COCK, DENNIS! And there was no phone number . . .

Recent advances in digital technology allow dead celebrities to endorse products that weren't even around when they were living. Just in case the heirs to my estate are getting any funny ideas, I want to get it out of the way right now: no matter what kind of cure for diarrhea they may discover in the year 2525, leave me the fuck out of it, all right?

I might not be most objective guy to lecture you on the dangers of pervasive consumerism, given my forays into the world of advertising, but please believe me: I am just as concerned as any of you about this problem, and try to take my warnings as a desperately needed wake-up call . . . of up to twenty minutes for only ninety-nine cents.

It's inescapable—from the designer label on the protruding elastic band of the size-52 underpants of the man in front of you in the line at Dunkin' Donuts straining to point out a maple cruller on the bottom rack of the display case to the drive to work during which you are subjected to a flashcard-like strobing of billboards that leave your brain stamped with subliminal impulses to fly United to Florida's Gulf Coast to take a Princess Cruise to a Radisson Hotel in the friendly Bahamas, where you'll drink Ronrico White Rum and wear an oversized Tommy Hilfiger shirt and Merrill hiking shoes while getting Lasik eye surgery, having your teeth whitened, getting approved for a home loan over the phone, and winning a large cash settlement for your personal injury claim. And then the light changes, and you drive a *second* block.

You know something? Life for me is just the downtime between Chevy "Like a Rock" ads, which have now officially lasted longer than Bob Seeger's career. Attention, Madison Avenue: I give up. You've won. Here's my wallet, just get it over with and paint milk mustaches on Mount Rushmore, okay?

Of course, that's just my opinion. I could be wrong.

Crime and Punishment

HE GOT THE SOFA
. . . AND THE CHAIR

Now, I don't want to get off on a rant here, but given our scant attention to victims' rights, sometimes victims are better off if the criminal is never caught. At least that way they only get fucked around once.

The volume of cases presently deluging the courts pretty much guarantees that no matter how heinous the crime, its victims are faceless entities, mere numbers on a court docket who are accorded all the dignity of a ring girl at a cockfight.

In order to avoid creating vigilantes, society takes the right of retribution for a crime away from the victim and makes it a matter for "the people." Of course, in America this means the solemn burden of justice is in the hands of the same people who created the Chia pet, order the "backyard wrestling" tapes, and have demanded seven distinct flavors of corn-nuts.

There's gotta be a way to protect the rights of victims. For example, victims should have a right to know when the animal who attacked them is going to get out of jail. They shouldn't have to read about it in the papers, or find out that their assailant took taxpayer-financed computer courses in prison and has just been hired as their boss.

And how about white-collar criminals who bilk people out of their life savings and are then given a slap on the wrist— sentenced to house arrest? The solution is simple: sentence them to house arrest in *their victim's* house. Trust me, they'll be beggin' for prison.

As for restitution, many criminals don't have any money. What they do have is unlimited time and limited space. I think they should have to spend their entire sentence pedaling a stationary bike in their cell that generates electricity and sends it to the home of their victims. Take a big chunk out of those monthly utility bills, huh?

I can't believe that there is any argument against rules requiring convicted child molesters to announce their presence in neighborhoods. I think they should have to wear bells on their shoes and a bright yellow windbreaker that says I AM A CONVICTED CHILD MOLESTER on the back, but I have a solution that should make everybody happy: let's force paroled child molesters to live in the same neighborhoods where all the ACLU attorneys live.

In the case of physical assault, the victim should have the right to choose his assailant's cellmate. If done properly, this could make the victim feel empowered, and the criminal feel vandalized. Or, at the very least, really sore.

In our increasingly vengeful society, guaranteeing crime victims their rights is not just desirable, it's essential. If we continue to push victims around, they may one day feel as if they have no choice but to take back their rights in the one way that they have seen work: by becoming defendants themselves.

Yes, we are all innocent until proven guilty, but when a self-confessed monster like Timothy McVeigh could stall his execution because of a few misplaced boxes of documents that only showed how much more guilty he was, we needed to get his ass up onto that gurney faster than the time it took for his scumbag lawyers to sign their upcoming book deals.

I endorsed the execution of Tim McVeigh. But every now and then, I felt a pang of guilt, thinking, "Could he have suffered more?" You know, in my fantasy, we get a Porta-John that's brimming with shit, we lock him in it, and we put the whole thing on a pickup truck driving slowly cross-country on badly paved roads.

Some anti–death penalty advocates say that McVeigh's execution didn't bring closure to the survivors of the bombing. Maybe not, but it did bring closure to McVeigh's eyes and, frankly, that's all I wanted.

Of course, that's just my opinion. I could be wrong.

Death

THE BIG SNOOZE

Talking about death and dying makes people feel about as comfortable as Shaquille O'Neal flying coach.

Now, I don't want to get off on a rant here, but death is the price we pay for life. Oh, by the way, I did see it much cheaper at Costco last weekend, so you might want to shop around.

We have a lot of cute euphemisms for death: "croaked," "kicked the bucket," "bought the farm," "took a dirt nap," "met your maker," "cashed in your chips," "ordered in from the dollar-an-item Mongolian barbecue in the alley behind the gold-chains-by-the-inch stand downtown."

There is a school of thought, usually promulgated by the topaz-jewelry-wearing, multiple-cat-owning, ancient-Volvo-with-

PRACTICE RANDOM KINDNESS AND SENSELESS ACTS OF

BEAUTY-bumper-sticker-driving segment of our population, that says we as a society need to remove the stigma from death and regard it as just another part of life. These rainbow-and-unicorn simpletons ask: "Why do we insist on portraying death as cruel?" Well, it's difficult to answer that question, but if I had to hazard a guess, I would say, *because it fucking kills us.*

Other cultures, perhaps those with less material wealth but a far richer spiritual heritage, embrace and celebrate death. But then, what do they have to live for in the first place? Of course you're gonna have a big bash for Grandpa Bo-ba-la, Bo-ba-la, Bo-ba-la when he goes. He doesn't have to eat dingo shit off a flat rock anymore.

Another thing I don't get is when a society decides it needs to keep the remains of a beloved leader on display. That's great, as long as they still admire you, but look what happened to Vladimir Lenin. Now they've got him standing up outside a Moscow discotheque, where parking valets pin car keys to his face.

It's ironic that in our culture everybody's biggest complaint is never having enough time, yet nothing terrifies us more than the idea of eternity. In America, we want to live forever, and a wide array of advanced cosmetic surgeries now guarantees that at least certain parts of us will. In fact, an increasing number of deceased bodies are now neither buried nor cremated, but returned for a deposit. Experts say that over the past twenty years, there's been a 72-percent increase in the number of eulogies that end in the phrase "nice rack."

Everyone who survives a near-death experience reports the same phenomenon: a bright light. You know what that is? It's the doctor, trying to detect any brain function by shining a flashlight into your pupils, you almost-dead clueless jagoff.

I hope there is no bright light. I don't want to go through eternity squinting. It will be hard enough to get laid in heaven—only the good girls are going up.

Some people feel the need to have bizarre funerals, trying to be the life of the party even when they're dead by insisting that everyone wear a Hawaiian shirt. These are the same assholes who get married on roller coasters. It's only a matter of time before some octogenarian prankster rigs his body to pop up out of the casket like Big Mouth Billy Bass and sing "Don't Worry—Be Happy."

The cost of dying is unbelievable, because just like in life, in death we can't resist having the latest and best of everything. Casket with Internet hook-up? Give me a break. When I go, stuff my ass full of candy and let some little Mexican kid whack me with a bat. I don't give a shit; I'm dead.

At my funeral, I want to have a TV screen showing the end of *The Beverly Hillbillies,* where they're all waving good-bye, but they have digitally superimposed my face over Granny's. Bury my heart at the cement pond.

I urge you to view your inevitable demise not with grief or fear but with acceptance and perhaps even hope. *Your* death is

Civil Disobedience

TO THE BARRICADES . . . IN SUVs

Now, I don't want to get off on a rant here, but the act of civil disobedience is deeply woven into the fabric of our nation. From the Boston Tea Party to the Beastie Boys' fight for your right to party, our country has a proud history of civil disobedience.

It has been a part of American history ever since the aforementioned plucky band of colonists refused to pay a tax on tea, thereby paving the way for a free, democratic nation that does not tax tea . . . except, of course, for a local sales tax paid by the purchaser, an income tax paid by the seller, and corporate taxes paid by the manufacturer . . .

Civil disobedience is the greatest engine for change the world has ever known.

However, all that today's so-called civil disobedients seem to be protesting is boredom and guilt over having well-off parents, while killing time between Dave Matthews's concerts.

Throwing a chair through the window of Starbucks because you disapprove of their treatment of coffee pickers in South America is juvenile. Throwing a chair through the window of Starbucks because you asked for a grande latte percent and they gave you a venti half-caf caramel macchiato, well, that's just common sense.

Do you know there are people who refuse to pay their federal income taxes because they don't want their money going toward building weapons of mass destruction? Now, while I applaud these citizens for their dedication to their ideals and for having the courage to act on their personal conscience, I also offer them one word of advice: *move*. It's a big world out there, Rainbow McDolphin. If you don't feel like paying the cover charge here at Club America, pack up your Birkenstocks and find yourself another place to groove, man.

Many participate in civil disobedience because it gives them an instant community of like-minded brethren who keep them from having to spend their evenings alone, perusing a three-year-old issue of *Mother Jones* magazine under the flickering half-light of that catshit-powered lamp in their hydroponic marijuana nursery, before crawling under their unbleached burlap sheets for the unsatisfying solace of a nongendered dildo carved out of a cruelty-free handmade beeswax candle.

Give them this, though: today's protesters are a lot more media-savvy than their predecessors, striving to spend more time in front of the camera than a lens cover. There are many people out there truly sacrificing for a worthy cause. However, I opine that for every one of them, there are many more who are in it for the publicity, the pussy, or the buzz.

I mean, look who's doing the protesting nowadays: garage-band dropouts, the chronically unemployed, limelight-whore politicians, and B-list entertainers looking for a career.

Remember that girl in the redwood tree? I think her name was Butterfly, and she was living there to keep a timber company from cutting it down. She stayed up in that tree for over a year through lightning storms and rain and fires. And, I have to say, I was inspired. So inspired, in fact, that about a week after hearing about Butterfly, when the owner of a local shoe store refused to give me a refund for what was obviously a defective pair of Hush Puppies, I got a sleeping bag and some basic supplies and climbed up in the green-striped canvas awning over the shoe store's front door. I read a book, took a nap, ate an olive-loaf sandwich, talked to some friends on my cell phone . . . then, an hour and a half later, climbed down and went home. I don't think the shoe-store owner ever even knew I was up there. But *I* knew it . . . and a few people walking by knew it . . . and I think sometimes you have to take a nap in other people's awnings, that's all.

Personal note to all the eco-zealots out there, inexplicably blocking the roads to protest global warming: you know nobody loves this planet more than I do. I live here, most of the time. But don't make me sit in traffic for six hours because the only way Mother Earth will let you fuck her is if I stop using hairspray.

In thirty years, this country has gone from Vietnam protesters poking flowers into the barrels of National Guardsmen's rifles to tossing over garbage cans and setting fire to police cars because we're *glad* the Lakers won the championship.

Ironically, nonviolent protest is at its most effective when it sparks the authorities into violence, shaming them in the eyes of the world. So, if you're a cop, and some irate malcontent dressed up like a sea turtle is screaming in your face about globalization or multinational corporations or whatever the latest code word is for "my parents say I have to be out of the house for at least four hours a day," well, pull out your billy club and give him a good whack on that so-many-piercings-you'd-think-it-was-a-fucking-tackle-box head of his. He'll be getting exactly what he wants. And if not, well, at least I will.

Of course, that's just my opinion. I could be wrong.

CALIFORNIA REAMIN'

Europeans seem to have little sympathy for California's current energy woes. I always find it a little grating when Germany refers to us as "power-hungry." We have windmills here in California, but we use them for miniature golf.

Now, I don't want to get off on a rant here, but the debate between environmentalists and energy advocates in this country shows no sign of abating, and, as a matter of fact, is only getting more confusing. You've got to love the philosophical clusterfuck that is a bicycle rack on a Lincoln Navigator.

This battle will no doubt be waged for years and years to come, largely because it's fueled by America's most plentiful natural resource: narrow-minded self-righteous indignation.

The state of California is currently bearing the brunt of the energy crisis, with rolling blackouts affecting vital services like hospitals, resulting in countless lopsided boob jobs. For the love of God, will the horror never end?

California doesn't have enough power plants because every time somebody tries to build one, someone finds a reason to stop it. Hey, you want to block a power plant because it might interfere with a migratory path for an albino duck gerbil? I cannot go along with that. We have to prioritize and decide what's really important here, people. You want to see animals thrive in their natural habitat? Go to the San Diego Zoo. I'm trying to microwave some popcorn over here, all right?

Maybe I'm in the minority on this, but my ideal vision of the world is one in which the only remaining species are somewhat literate human beings and small, well-mannered beagles wearing little top hats and bow ties.

The oil companies want to drill in the Arctic National Wildlife Refuge, but the environmentalists say it places in jeopardy a prime breeding ground for Alaskan caribou. I have to pay four bucks a gallon just so Donner and Blitzen can get their rocks off? I say we don't touch the oil reserves and just invent a car that runs on *endangered species*, okay? Put a tiger in your tank. Literally.

If we are to maintain our position as a world power, we must dedicate ourselves to finding acceptable alternatives to fossil fuels. Wind power and solar power are clean, cheap, safe, renewable sources of energy, which, I believe, will be widely used as soon as someone figures out how to establish a price-gouging monopoly on them.

I'm a big proponent of alternative energy. As a matter of fact, at this very moment, every single watt of electricity in my home is being provided by an alternative energy source: a low-cost, underground shunt-wire that my brother-in-law David has tapped into my next-door neighbor's fuse box. It's cut my bill in half.

At my house, everyone is aware of the energy crisis, and we all pitch in to do our part. For example, I never use the twin Boeing 747 engines I bought to run my Dancing Waters Lagoon while running my Bumper Boats at the same time. That just wouldn't be fair.

Another way I do my part is by going down to the ride-share station in my neighborhood and inviting a complete stranger to get inside my car so we can qualify for the carpool lane. It shaves about forty-five minutes off my commute, and sometimes, if I'm lucky, the stranger will hold a gun to my head and force me to blow him.

I may pretend not to care about what happens thousands of miles away in a place I'll probably never see, but I know that all of life is interconnected in a symbiotic, primal dance. That a butterfly beating its wings in the African bush can dislodge a particle of dust that makes a monkey sneeze, that startles a herd of gazelles into stampeding, causing a rockslide down a hill that dams up a stream and floods it, creating moisture that evaporates and cools the air, that rushes into the hot air above it, becoming a cyclone, that whirls out to sea and joins up with other storm clouds, forming an enormous raging squall that travels thousands of miles across the ocean, disrupting electromagnetic fields and making *my* cell phone cut out. Fuckin' butterflies.

Of course, that's just my opinion. I could be wrong.

DON'T PANIC . . . OOPS, YOU'RE RIGHT, PANIC

Now, I don't want to get off on a rant here, but to me, anxiety makes sense. I see it as a reasonable response to the frightening clusterfuck that is our increasingly stressful world. The people who creep me out are the ones who don't seem to be bothered by anything. My theory is that anybody who has it completely together in times like these is either stupid, crazy, or *evil*.

Mental-health professionals believe anxiety stems from not facing your true emotional needs. That's why psychiatrists advise you to uncover those hidden fears you dare not name—because then, and only then, can you stop being anxious and start being completely fucking insane, and that's where the real money is.

Over the last decade, pagers, cell phones, and personal digital assistants have marionetted us into a Sisyphean existence where we are perpetually ten minutes late for our next appointment. The only reason we're living longer nowadays is because we can't fit death into our schedules anymore. Anybody remember a simpler time when "Palm Pilot" was just a nickname your friends gave you when you hit puberty?

Youth-obsessed, money-hungry, power-grabbing Los Angeles is Ground Xanax for anxiety. You see it in the clenched jaw of the high-strung B-movie producer who's wrestling his Humvee into the handicapped parking spot so he can get to his meditation class on time.

Anxiety can lead to phobias such as fear of strangers, fear of elevators, fear of airplanes, fear of heights, fear of speaking in public, and fear of parties. *Got it, got it, need it, got it, need it, got it.*

Some guys suffer from urination anxiety: the presence of other men acts like a psychological truck parked on top of their personal garden-hose. I have the reverse problem: I can only pee when somebody else is watching. So if you ever run into me in a restroom, and I've got a sock puppet over my free hand, and I'm saying in a squeaky voice, "I can see your wee wee, Dennis!"— well, I'm not a freak. That is a prescription sock puppet.

Psychiatrists claim that some men fear having sex because they subconsciously fear the woman is about to devour their penis. I was always afraid she might get it stuck between her teeth.

People deal with anxiety in different ways: some take yoga, some take tai chi, others work it off in the gym. Me? Once a month or so, I take off all my clothes, climb on my candy-apple-red moped, and drive really fast into a field of corn. And as the stalks and ears of caressing maize batter my exposed flesh, I suddenly feel my other problems melting away. Sure, it means coming home in the backseat of a police car with a blanket draped over my head and shoulders, but, sorry, kids, Daddy needs his "Me Time."

If you suffer from chronic anxiety, repeated panic attacks, obsessions, compulsions or social phobias, take my advice: forget therapy and don't even think about drugs. I know it sounds crazy, but my sanctuary has always been the Laundromat. Think about it. You immerse yourself in the calming hum of the washing machines, the familiar warmth emanating from the dryers, the comforting smell of soap, and the soothing snap and pleasant pop of loving mothers folding clean sheets. Relax in the un-competitive, undemanding realm of vending machines that feature off-brand sodas and circus peanuts. Self-conscious about your appearance? Just take a look around. You're a prince. Socially awkward? Well, anything short of flinging fecal matter at the change lady, and you're a charmer in this quirky little kingdom. Obsessive-compulsive? Hey, go ahead. Count quarters until your fingers bleed. Sexually frustrated? Well, just collect the thick wads of lint from all the dryers and fashion them into a large

LIVING AND DYING IN TRIPLICATE

Now, I don't want to get off on a rant here, but bureaucracy is out of control. Bureaucracy is out of control. Bureaucracy is out of control. They told me I had to give you that in triplicate. You know, we live in a society where it's easier to climb back into the birth canal than it is to get a copy of your birth certificate.

Bureaucracy. Just take a look at the word. I mean, how come there's no *O*? It sounds like there should be an *O*, but instead there's an *E*, an *A*, and a *U*. Of course, the sensible thing to do would be to eliminate those unnecessary letters and just replace them with the *O*, but it can't be done because the *E* has tenure, the *A* is the union shop steward, and the *U* is married to the boss's accountant's son.

I'd be perfectly fine with all the rules and red tape if we didn't have to wait in line for so long that the people in the line eventually develop their own regional dialect. Do you really think it's just a coincidence that government offices have the birth and death registries in the same room?

I can't even clean up after my dog now without first getting an environmental-impact statement from the Army Corps of Engineers. It's gotten so bad that I now demand to see three forms of ID before I'll let me pleasure myself in the shower.

And is there any pus-pocket of perdition more soul-destroying than the Department of Motor Vehicles? People go in whistling like Andy Griffith skipping rocks and they leave more pissed off than Gary Condit's wife. In exchange for the privilege of operating an automobile, you have to embark on a Hieronymus Bosch–like odyssey through the dingy, institutional-green, cinderblock-lined bowels of the System at its most wearisome. First, you find the line for the people who have appointments; then you wait for them to call your name; then you get in another line for people with your blood type and birth date; then the clerk who's been taking people in your line goes to lunch, so you have to line up at another window; then, after several evolutionary epochs during which innumerable species have arisen, roamed the earth, and then succumbed to extinction, you finally reach the front of the line, where the whole process culminates in your challenging Death to a chess match.

I discovered one of the more frustrating strains of bureaucracy recently when I applied for a mortgage. Hey, all I want is to borrow some money and pay you back five times the amount over the next thirty years. If I don't pay it back, you keep the house and my money. Why you fuckin' with me?

What is particularly exasperating about bureaucracy is that you can never put a face or a name to the logjam. The genius of bureaucracy is it's never one person's fault—it's everyone's. It's ineptitude in its most socialistic form. Whenever you walk into a store that proudly stresses teamwork, save yourself some time and money and just back your naked ass up to the Ream-A-Tron.

The reason bureaucracies metastasize the way they do nowa-days is that when you try to fire someone, they automatically sue you. So now it's easier to just give them a desk and say, "Don't touch anything," and then tell everyone what a great job they're doing, in the hopes that your competitor will eventually steal them away from you.

Ah, the bureaucrat. A murky figure, smelling slightly of fax toner, for whom you must constantly tack back and forth between sympathy and white-hot antipathy. Sure, there are plenty of them out there who are hardworking and conscientious and friendly. But there are just as many who have used their hummingbird's teardrop of power to build a tiny administrative empire out of policies and waiting lists and access to files, so that—for the two to four hours a day they're actually working—they may bestride the rest of us like some kind of Cubicle Colossus bellowing, "I am Ozymandias, Clerk of Clerks! Look on my Files, ye Mighty, and despair! All ye who enter here."

Face it: we might complain bitterly about bureaucracy and red tape, but at least they give us something to blame when our lives don't go exactly the way we want them to. There is something soothing about the abdication of responsibility, the Zen-like moment when you give up and see the poetry in the ticket agent's telling you that not only does your flight reservation not exist but you're going to be charged for the ticket anyway, the moment when the college-admission board notifies you that your grade-point average is too *high* to qualify for a scholarship, or the moment a Veteran Administration's official tells you to your face that you died in combat over thirty years ago. Lose yourself in the arcane maze of nonsensical rules, delight in the Lewis Carroll–like anarchy of the organizational world. In other words, relax and take it easy, because if you do flip out and have to be committed to the nuthouse, you would not believe the fuckin' paperwork involved.

Of course, that's just my opinion. I could be wrong.

Marriage

WEDDING DISS

The White House is looking into a plan that would allow illegal immigrants to stay in the United States. The plan calls for a million Mexicans to marry a million of our ugliest citizens. Just trying to make everyone happy.

Now, I don't want to get off on a rant here, but no matter how much it has changed, marriage is a vital cog in our societal machine. Dating's fine, living together is great, but anyone who's truly in love eventually looks at his or her partner and thinks, "I want to cut down on having sex with this person and get on their insurance plan."

Are marriages failing, or are people simply living longer and finding that they can't stay with the same person for that long? The answer is, marriages are failing. You know your marriage is in trouble when your wife starts wearing the wedding ring on her middle finger. In Hollywood, you can get a marriage license printed on an Etch A Sketch.

Until recently, television was notorious for romanticizing bachelorhood while making vague insinuations about the sexuality of the "unattached woman." Magnum, P.I., got more ass than a rental car, while Laverne actually had a scarlet *L* sewn onto her sweater.

It seems as though every wedding nowadays has to be "themed." There are period-costume weddings. Elvis weddings. Fairy-tale weddings. Weddings so unbelievably complicated and elaborate, the only way you can tell who's actually getting married is to find the couple fucking in the coatroom . . . and ask them who they're the best man and maid of honor for.

If you want to truly understand how complex marriage has become, simply ask the people on the front lines: the ones who make up the wedding invitations. They are constantly trying to skirt around the gender, age, and parental issues and still get paid: "Mona Johnson and her life partner, Brianne, invite you to the wedding of their son Lars and his lover, Oswaldo, with the blessing of their surrogate daughter Quan, where they will be married by their Shaman, Ali Ben Shapiro, in Carlsbad Caverns on the eve of the summer solstice, to be followed by an all-vegan luau, featuring the music of two members of Kansas. Dress is casual-Friday-meets-'80s-disco. No furs. The couple is registered at Nordstrom and Zach's House of Knobby Dildoes."

Straight couples have been breaking their vows for years, but gay couples are still fighting to gain that right. Gay unions are now legal in a state like Vermont, but are not having much luck in the South, where there are strict rules that forbid getting married unless you are heterosexual, fourteen, or "kin."

I once went to a lesbian wedding ceremony between my wife's former hairstylist, a lovely thirty-year-old woman, and her partner, a very hot dental hygienist in her mid-twenties. The wedding was small and simple. The reception was warm and friendly. And from what I could see from my surveillance hammock in the branches of a tree high outside the third floor of the Laguna Beach Hilton, the wedding night was, well, not nearly kinky enough.

You know, never ever discount the idea of marriage. Sure, someone might tell you that marriage is just a piece of paper. Well, so is money, and what's more life-affirming than cold, hard cash?

The most difficult thing about marriage for men is that they know they shouldn't get married unless they're mature, but feel they can't become mature unless they get married. I'm not sure I know what the answer is, other than I'm pretty sure it's a bad idea to fuck the stripper at your bachelor party.

Guys should never whine about marriage, because guys are no prize, especially when we get older. I was at the post office last week, and standing in front of me was some guy in his mid-seventies. He was wearing a powder-blue polyester shirt more pilled than a nightstand at Graceland, and he was dusted with so much dandruff, I was tempted to place Christmas Village figurines on his shoulders. He was also wearing a cap with the phrase ASK ME ABOUT MY PROSTATE on it, and off-white slacks with a white belt, and there was a large pee spot near his left knee. And you wanna know the most shocking part of his ensemble? He was wearing a wedding ring. The one that I placed on his finger a scant two years ago. I love you, pappy!

Of course, that's just my opinion. I could be wrong.

Why Football Has Replaced Baseball as the National Pastime

"WELL, ISN'T IT OBVIOUS?"

Now, I don't want to get off on a rant here, but it's obvious to me that football has replaced baseball as our national pastime. Other countries have their pastimes. Canada has hockey. China has Ping-Pong. Europe has killing each other over a bad call at a soccer game. And we have the NFL! Baseball is a reflection of how we think America might have been, while football mirrors exactly how it really is. Football says more about America, because it represents that perfect fusion of brawn and brain.

The idea that baseball could be our nation's pastime says less about the game and more about the need for Americans to stay on this de Tocquevillian quest to unlock who we are as a people. Baseball doesn't say any more about us than jazz, slavery, or our love affair with the automobile do. Baseball is an adorable little game that Americans invented when they had both the time and the space. But now time and space are in shorter supply and we crave a game like football that reflects that.

Truth be told, baseball is slower that George W. Bush trying to master trigonometry. Many people think baseball is a metaphor for life. What I want to know is whose life are they talking about? Last time I checked, life didn't seem to last for an eternity. Life is short; baseball goes on forever.

Let's face it, not much happens in baseball. Abner Doubleday gets credited with inventing the game, but Harold Pinter was the one who did punch up. The only thing worse than a bad baseball game is realizing that you have to stay until everybody leaves because you can't remember where you parked.

If I had to pinpoint the exact moment when football surpassed baseball as our nation's pastime it was when Don Zimmer became coach and took the field in his Yankee pinstripes. The guy looked like a bratwurst. Football coaches wear jackets because they're smart enough to know that there comes a time in a man's life when gravity, beer, and marshmallows have finally won and you look like an idiot trying to squeeze into your Little League outfit.

Baseball is the game we associate with spring. But with the ever-increasing greenhouse effect, the thought of warmer weather doesn't stir us the way it once did. Football, on the other hand, reminds us of a gentler, more innocent America quickly vanishing, one of icy autumn's shivers, blinding snows, and the Donner party.

The more diverse the game of baseball becomes, the more homogenized it all seems to feel. Teams no longer reflect the city they come from but rather the agents who were able to make the better deal. Before free agency, you could see the Yankees play one season and come back the next, and pretty much expect to see the same players. But things have changed. I actually went to a game where Jose Canseco batted for the Oakland As in the first inning and the Yankees in the fifth, because he had been traded.

Football understands implicitly that if they don't hang together they hang separately.

The essential problem with baseball is that teams able to garner huge television contracts in big markets like Los Angeles or New York are now able to dominate the game by buying the best players. Unlike football, which, along with salary caps, pools television revenues allowing each team to put together rosters that are evenly matched, in baseball the spoils now go to those lucky enough to be in larger cities. How ironic that football, the seemingly more brutish sport so rooted in society's Darwinian underbelly, would recognize the importance of sharing in order to survive. Football knows that competition is important, but only between the players, not the team owners.

But these are all just sidebar issues. The real, core reason that baseball is glimpsing football's roadrunner cloud heading off into the distance is that football isn't just a better, more fan-friendly game. It's the happy-to-see-you family dog, while baseball is the maybe-you'll-be-lucky-and-I'll-let-you-pet-me cat.

Baseball is a George Will doodle. Football is the arena. Circus Maximus. The dramatic weekly build to a concussive game played by brave men. The spectacle is enhanced by the fact that 99.99999 percent of us know we can't go there. Baseball? Well, most of us have played softball. Sometimes drunk. Our baseball fantasies often star ourselves. But tackle football. Forget it. Get some Bugles and park it on the couch, it's time for the big guys to show you how it's done.

I do have one suggestion for baseball if they want to get back into the hunt. There's a lot of unused space in the alley between right and center field. Why not have a football game going on out there to keep the fans occupied during some of the longer lulls in the baseball game.

Of course, that's just my opinion. I could be wrong.

The Super Bowl

"THE MAIN EVENT"

If everything falls the right way, I will be in the broadcast booth for next season's Super Bowl and that will certainly be one of the biggest thrills of my life. Other than a hardcore group of holdout curling zealots in Flin Flon, Canada, most would agree that the Super Bowl is the number-one spectacle in the entire world of sports.

Now, I don't want to get off on a rant here, but did you see last year's game? Last year's Super Bowl saw an incredible display of brute strength, passionate agility, and machismo swagger that only comes from a lifelong commitment to excellence. But that's to be expected when 'N Sync and the Backstreet Boys are forced to share the same dressing room.

Hard to believe the Super Bowl is turning XXXVI. It seems like just yesterday I was thinking, "Boy, this Namath kid is just beggin' for an ass-kicking." But Joe Willie pulled the sword from the stone and the rest is history.

I love everything about the Super Bowl. The preshow, the preshow preview, the kickoff, the halftime show, the commercials, the postgame preview, the postgame show, the postgame wrap-up featuring highlights from the postgame preview, and then, of course, my favorite: the preview of next year's Super Bowl wrap-up.

It means a lot to win the Super Bowl. If you win, you end up getting a call from the president. If you lose you also get a call from the president because he's not too good at dialing yet.

The night before Super Bowl Sunday I can never sleep because of all that excitement building up to it. Sharing the day with friends and family. The food, the drink, the all-around good spirits. I make Super Bowl a really important time in my life because growing up, well, we didn't have Super Bowl Sunday. Interleague play was frowned upon back then. But why burden you with my problems.

The Super Bowl is everybody's favorite day of the year. But none more so than Gary Condit's, because that's the only day of the year he has a chance of maybe getting a table at Le Cirque.

The actual name Super Bowl was invented by Kansas City Chiefs owner Lamar Hunt. Lamar also came up with the names Gynomotrin, Allerest, and Pringles. He's got a special gift when it comes to those kinds of things.

Probably the one name that stands out more than anybody else's is Joe Montana. Montana won four, with everyone remembering Super Bowl XXIII, in which he beat the Bengals in a 92-yard scoring drive with only 26 seconds left to play. The only time I screamed more during a Super Bowl was last year when the caterer ran out of hummus before the end of the first quarter.

While the huge event status of the Super Bowl never wanes, sometimes the games have been very one-sided. Some Super Bowls are over before the first quarter is even done. Super Bowl XX, for example, between the Bears and the Patriots, was over before Super Bowl XIX began.

I also don't think we make enough use of the two weeks in between the end of the AFC and NFC championship playoffs and the start of the Super Bowl. There should be some sort of game in between to keep our attention. I'm thinking we put together a cross-genre game where the best football players in the league go up against the best baseball players in a game of football, and then, if any of the baseball players can still move, we can have a go at their poetic little endeavor.

The horse is out of the barn. The Super Bowl has moved way beyond game status—it's a cultural touchstone. More toilets are flushed during Super Bowl halftime than at any other time of the year. Which brings me to my next point. It's really not a La-Z-Boy if there's no tubing running from the chair to a septic tank near the garden, now is it?

Here's a little tip: the best time to go to Sea World or Knotts Berry Farm is during the Super Bowl. The place is completely empty because everyone is home watching. Including the college kids who operate the rides. But it's still nice to see what the place would be like if you could do something there.

As big as the game is, some people sometimes give it a little too much importance. There is a school of economic science, for example, that believes the Super Bowl is actually an indicator of how the stock market will do for the remainder of the year. The theory maintains that if any team from the original NFL wins, the stock market goes up, while if a team from the old AFL wins—it goes down. Idiots. Everyone knows the only way to predict the market is by tracking down Chuck Woolery and measuring his sideburns.

Super Bowl Sunday is the one day of the year where everyone in the country, regardless of their religious beliefs, completely stops what they're normally doing. Especially the team I'm rooting for.

When I was younger, I thought there could be no greater status symbol than owning tickets to the Super Bowl. Now that I'm older, I realize you really need to own the winning team. Or maybe even announce the game.

It's the Big Kahuna. Thirteen million pounds of guacamole and 8.5 million pounds of tortilla chips. But enough about Pavarotti watching the game alone. Let's talk about sports.

Of course, that's just my opinion. I could be wrong.

WRESTLING WITH YOUR SUBCONSCIOUS

Now, I don't want to get off on a rant here, but the XFL was so horrible, viewers jammed the NBC switchboards, angrily demanding that the network start running the movie *Heidi*. As a matter of fact, toward the very end, NBC tried turning this Hindenburg-sized catastrophe into a positive by using it as a vehicle to cross-promote their competitor's programs.

The XFL went from some of the highest ratings of the season to being the least-watched show in television history. It kinda reminded me of President Bush's huge approval rating right after the Gulf War, which turned into a defeat at Bill Clinton's hands a year later. The XFL had violated one of the cardinal rules of television: you can't promise not to raise expectations and then go ahead and lower them.

The other day the guy from the Salvation Army came to pick up my old big-screen television. He and his buddy were halfway out of the house and near the truck when they stopped dead in their tracks and said in an accusatory tone that they could tell I had watched the XFL on it and had a lot of nerve trying to pass it off on some unsuspecting adult. After I apologized profusely by throwing them wads of cash, they agreed to help me bury it in the backyard, but no matter how much dirt we threw over the television, we couldn't seem to dampen the bright, fiery-red glow that seemed to emanate from deep within the earth's molten bowels.

Look, I'm not one of those football purists who believe the rules of the game were etched on clay tablets with bolts of lightning from Mount Olympus. Evolution is not only good but necessary for the game's survival. But the XFL was a ten-yard penalty back into the primordial ooze. It wasn't even so bad that it was bad in a fun way. It was just bad.

At first the ratings were tremendous, so you saw advertisers like the U.S. Army, Snickers, and Budweiser. But near the end they were running commercials for Blinky's Technical College, as well as personal appeals from some of the network executives asking if anyone had a spare attic they could hide in till this thing blew over. I saw commercials for ValueJet, Pets.com, and "Nixon. Now More Than Ever."

NBC was desperate, because they hadn't had a major hit on Saturday night since *The Golden Girls*. But that was still no reason for Estelle Getty, Rue McClanahan, and Betty White to suit up and play secondary for the New York Hitmen. They could have been seriously injured. Although, I gotta say, Bea Arthur, when she stays focused, can really protect the pocket.

This was a 150-million-dollar Pentagon-procurement-sized blunder. And as long as you don't own stock in the WWF, it's somewhat reassuring to discover that you *can* go broke underestimating the intelligence of the American people. As a matter of fact, the television executive who green-lit *Supertrain* finally found the confidence to pop his head out of the pit to ask if it was safe now to apologize.

The XFL married football to wrestling. Have we not learned anything from Pamela and Tommy Lee?

The XFL had its roots more in the WWF than it did in the NFL. The difference between the XFL and the WWF is that the WWF is completely scripted whereas the XFL played actual games in which nobody knew the outcome—ever. That's because by the time the game was finished everyone had stopped watching, including the guy paid to work the scoreboard.

The XFL tried to appeal to NFL fans who were tired of watching football players performing at the top of their game. Vince McMahon surveyed the market and realized that what Americans truly wanted was really, really bad football. The kind of football where viewers can't even tell if that's a football game going on or just some scantily clad women cheering for a trash-talking midget antelope giving birth to a dented tool box on the Discovery Channel.

Overnight Vince McMahon went from presenting the WWF, a show that was fixed, to the XFL, which was irreparably broken, and the fact that the cheerleaders were way too provocative, I felt, took away from the activities on the field. I saw one game where a player was called for holding, and he was standing by himself.

I myself enjoyed watching the game, because I liked to keep track of the number of times they cut to a cheerleader and then someone in the booth piped in with, "And speaking of tight ends in the scoring position." Then they all had a knowing laugh, like Robert Benchley whispering something deliciously salacious into Dorothy Parker's ear as Frances Marion enters the bar.

Hey, I don't mind Jesse Ventura being governor. But when he thinks he can announce pro football, well, now you're trampling on something I consider sacred. The guy I felt sorry for was announcer Matt Vasgersian. He was just in under his head. Halfway through the first game he grabbed the Telestrator pen and began scribbling the words HELP ME.

And I also felt really sorry for the players. I saw one game where a receiver caught the ball, ran into the end zone, took off his helmet, and kept running through the stands, into the parking lot, and into a cab. Last time I heard, he had plastic surgery, changed his name, and was living somewhere in the mountains outside of Macchu Pichu.

Needless to say, the league began to hemorrhage money. That's why they had that scramble for the ball at the beginning of the game . . . they had no coin to toss.

A sure sign that your league is about to go under is when right before kickoff the commissioner makes a personal appeal to the players individually, begging them to "take it easy on the grass."

How can I describe the XFL for those of you who might have missed it? Well, let's see. Imagine *Rififi* without the heist, *West Side Story* without Bernstein's soundtrack, or tennis without the ball, net, racquet, or players.

Thirteen of the NFL's thirty-one teams got their start in other leagues. So, who knows, maybe some of these XFL teams like the Hitmen, and the Thunderbolts, or the Maniax, will someday find their way into the Big Time. And maybe I can eat so many Turkey Jerkies in one sitting that I'll have so much gas I can achieve liftoff.

Of course, that's just my opinion. I could be wrong.

Fans

YOU'RE NO. 1!
YOU'RE NO. 1!

I am a fan of the fans. At times, during my inaugural season on *Monday Night Football*, I was pilloried in the daily press, but the fans were always nice to me, even when they weren't particularly fond of what I was doing at that time. They'd tell me to hang in there and as the latter part of the season rolled around and I had progressed in the job, a lot of them gave me a thumbs-up. It was much appreciated.

Now that I've written the longest uninterrupted nice paragraph in the history of the rants, it's time to consider fandom in general.

Now, I don't want to get off on a rant here, but it's not easy to be a fan anymore these days. You have to really want it. In exchange for lacquering your very being with more home team–colored body paint than a $99 special at Earl Scheib's, you're submitted to a battery of loyalty tests that no other fans in history had to navigate.

I took my kids to a Lakers game last season, and by the time I was done paying for parking, nachos, and a Chuck Hearn blowup doll, it might have been cheaper to just buy the team.

Prices for Lakers tickets have gotten astronomical. During the playoffs, there was a scalper standing outside Staples Center who wanted to charge me six hundred bucks *not* to see the game. It was right before tip-off so I was able to knock it down to five hundred and fifty. Ended up being an amazing game. Sorry I missed it.

And even increased ticket prices don't ensure stability for the fans. George Steinbrenner has been threatening to move out more often than Tommy and Pamela Lee. You know what, George? Go someplace else, if you think there's another city on this planet besides New York that would put up with your unremitting torrential monsoon of bullshit. And this is coming from a devoted fan who truly admires the guy.

New York fans are, of course, legendary. In fact, they're so enthusiastic that police actually built a jail underneath Shea Stadium just in case a couple of the fans get too out of hand, or Darryl Strawberry thinks it might be time for another comeback. Actually, that's not so bad when you consider that the Texas Rangers keep a jail *and* an electric chair set on "simmer."

New York fans are, without a doubt, the most loyal, but when you let them down they can be surly. In some towns, fans show their dismay by throwing snowballs with batteries inside of them, hot dogs, even chairs. I have been to games in New York where the fans literally lopped off their own heads and threw them at the players.

Los Angeles fans couldn't seem any more jaded if they were modeling Badgley Mischka. Give you an idea how indifferent L.A. fans are. The Rams moved to St. Louis years ago, and half the season-ticket holders in this town are still renewing each year.

The worst fans in the world have to be at cockfights. I was in Oklahoma the other weekend and I attended a cockfight, and there was a guy who completely ignored the NO SMOKING sign. Granted, we were in a skybox, but still, cockfight arenas tend to be intimate and his cigar smoke was blowing right toward the ring. I tried to explain that these cocks need to be at peak performance levels and high concentrations of nicotine and tar get them off their game. The guy just looked at me through his good eye as if daring me to call cockfight security.

Golf has the world's most polite fans, but that's only because they're exhausted from going hole-to-hole and getting more exercise than the guys actually playing it.

Say what you will about American fans. Why are we always told that European soccer fans are the world's greatest? Bleachers collapsing, stampedes, people dying from getting bonked in the throat by tear-gas canisters fired up by riot police? A group of British barristers recently denounced the U.S. for its continued use of the death penalty in the McVeigh case. The Brits said there is absolutely no reason for a human being to take another human being's life . . . unless, of course, their team happens to beat yours at soccer.

The most exasperating thing about being a fan is that girls have it so much easier than guys when it comes to hanging with the players. There are gals who can't tell the difference between a hockey stick and a polo mallet, but because they're willing to wrestle naked with another woman in the back room of an Atlanta strip joint while guys shine flashlights, they get to hang with some of America's greatest players. Meanwhile, someone who really appreciates the game, someone who could have a meaningful conversation with the same player about the subtle nuances of man-to-man versus zone and what he might have done wrong last Sunday—not only can't I get into the back room in there with him, I'm told to leave because I'm scaring the paying customers.

So let's hear it for the fans! It's not easy to hoist yourself up out of the Barcalounger and head off to the stadium when many of the games are now on TV in the first place. And while we're on the subject, what's the story with the urinals at stadiums? What's with that bathtub with six pounds of ice in it? I can't tell if I'm supposed to take a leak or jump in there and break a fever.

Of course, that's just my opinion. I could be wrong.

FIRST-TIME CALLER, LONG-TIME RANTER

I was thumbing through this morning's sports pages and I see that one of my favorite pundits feels that Barry Bonds is a bit on the surly side. Really? Maybe he'd be a little nicer if you left him the fuck alone and just let him do his job.

Now, I don't want to get off on a rant here, but in the world of sports there are the winners and then there are the losers, and then, increasingly, there are those who earn their living writing or talking about it.

I'm not saying everyone in the sports-punditry business is an idiot. I believe I'm in there somewhere, and I'm sure *I'm* not everybody's cup of tea.

What I'm talking about is the four-hundred-pound sports-talk radio host who, in between mouthfuls of corned-beef sandwiches and mayonnaise salad washed down with a glass of pureed Snicker bars, says he thinks Derek Jeter's starting to get a little soft.

I'm talking about the local six-P.M. TV-sports guy in the comfort zone of a television studio, wearing a wig that couldn't be any more obvious if it were a tribble from *Star Trek,* calling Tiger Woods a whiner for even mentioning the wind at the British Open.

Don't misunderstand me. Sports punditry is fun, it enhances the game, and there's something cute as well as cathartic about getting worked up over things that really don't matter. It's the safety valve that lets us get off some steam without addressing the truly important issues that bother us, like unaffordable housing, FBI screw-ups, and what's to make of the ending of the remake of *Planet of the Apes.*

Many of the fans and some of the pundits have forged an unholy alliance blowing the significance of players and coaches and their mistakes way out of proportion. We are losing sight of the fact that sports should always be a diversion from life's travails and not the cause of it. If Rondell White's getting sent down to the minors is making you sound like the final days of the Woodrow Wilson administration, then you really need to start monitoring the frequency of your erections.

You know, it's a sad commentary on the current state of government when the most heated opinions in America are over whether or not Bill Mazeroski's .260 lifetime batting average should have kept him out of the Hall of Fame, and not what should be listed in a comprehensive Patient's Bill of Rights. Oh, by the way, one of those rights: while giving me a prostate exam, the doctor shouldn't be asking me whom I like in the Cotton Bowl.

Sportswriters are the ones who determine who gets the Cy Young as well as the Most Valuable Player Award. So, obviously, these guys carry a lot of weight, and I don't just mean their midsections. And some abuse that weight.

There are a lot of great sportswriters out there who breathe life into the game for those of us who didn't see it. What I'm talking about is the guy who missed Mark McGwire swatting Roger Maris's record out of the park because he was too busy checking to see if there were any more of those cool-looking free ESPN tote bags left in the media center.

Some of the greatest writers of the twentieth century have been reporters who covered sports. Red Smith, Ring Lardner, Damon Runyon, and, of course, Grantland Rice. A day doesn't go by that I don't mean to read some of them.

The dean of sportswriters was a man named Grantland Rice. Rice brought a level of literacy to the field that so many of today's writers aim for but so often miss the mark. Rice is responsible for possibly the most famous opening paragraph in the history of sportswriting. The year was 1932, the game was the Rose Bowl. The paragraph: "Maybe my ass was burning from last night's chili, but it didn't matter, because from the moment of kickoff I was on my feet." Ah, they just don't turn a phrase like that these days.

Damon Runyon not only covered sports but wrote fiction. Many of you have probably heard the term "Runyonesque" but have no idea what it means. Well, it means to be like something Damon Runyon wrote about. Glad I could be of service.

Ring Lardner didn't just recount the game, he covered the personalities on and off the field. When you read Ring Lardner you smelled the stadium, tasted the hot dog, heard the crowd. In other words, you really had to do a lot of skimming to find out what the fucking score was.

I happen to be a huge fan of sports-talk radio. I find it somehow reassuring that with Third World debt crippling emerging economies, ethnic bloodshed, global warming, and the outbreak of hepatitis C, there are still people in this world who can get suicidal over the fact that the Philadelphia Eagles haven't beaten the Giants since '97.

I call sports-talk radio all the time. Maybe you're familiar with my work. I'm the guy who can't seem to figure out how to turn his radio down.

Most of the callers on sports-talk radio that I hear often have cogent points to make and frequently do so in a surprisingly funny manner. But some of these guys are just plain scary.

Some of the people who call talk radio already have a built-in seven-second delay in their head. Every time I listen to these particular callers, the same identical thought occurs to me: you know, maybe the electoral college is a good idea after all.

But overall, I like the new wave of sports punditry. Indeed, I am a lucky recipient of the fruits of its proliferation.

What I object to is the sports-pundit-turned-bully. The lucky hack enjoying his first blush of power only capable of substituting vitriol for talent while cringing in fear at even the thought of someone turning the tables and eviscerating him. You know the type. The no-talent half-wit who can neither dish it out nor take it.

Sports-talk radio is too often a lethal concoction of ego and bravado masking a deep-rooted insecurity. That doesn't mean I don't love it. In fact, that's exactly why I love it. But I'm also aware that it takes a huge chunk out of my day, time that could otherwise be spent doing something a little more productive. You know, like watching sports-talk television with my family.

Of course, that's just my opinion. I could be wrong.

JUST THE TIP
OF THE VICE-BERG

Now, I don't want to get off on a rant here, but if they didn't want Washington to be a hotbed of sexual activity, they shouldn't have named it after the guy who fathered the entire country. What else would you expect from a town that's famed for its cherry blossoms?

Sex has served as the you-don't-want-to-know-where-it's-been coin of the realm in American politics long before the Clintons and Condits came along. Thomas Jefferson is said to have sired a child by one of his slaves, and I wouldn't be surprised if the original George W. left a set of those wooden teeth on the wrong nightstand now and then. Let's face it: there's constant groping going on in our nation's capital even when George Bush *isn't* trying to find the right word.

Do I think power corrupted Gary Condit? No. You can't blame Congress for turning him into something he already was. Gary Condit is simply a skivvy hound using the illusion of power to get laid. If Condit wasn't a congressman, he'd be working as a car salesman who appears in his own TV commercials trying to nail female customers with the same mix of low-rent celebrity and bullshit power by telling them he's John Davidson's half-brother and he can "do something" for them on the undercoating package.

It's guys like Condit who usually make me side with the women in these libidinal conflagrations. Everyone criticized Monica Lewinsky for being so indiscreet about blowing the president, but come on: what's the point of blowing the president if you can't tell everyone you blew the president? You know, there have only been forty-two of those cocks and you had one of them lodged in your noggin. Why not take out an ad in the trades?

I don't believe there's any danger of a sex scandal with our current administration. President Bush not only appears to be deeply in love with his wife, he thinks "fetish" is something you crumble on top of a Greek salad. And as for Dick Cheney, well, his team of doctors has cautioned him to not even look at a bra ad, much less fuck.

More disturbing than the sex scandals that emanate from Washington, D.C., is the realization that they are merely the tip of the vice-berg. Our form of government is like a recipe for kink: take some jagoff in a clip-on tie who under any other circumstances couldn't get laid if his penis had its own vagina, send him far away from his bowling-trophy wife for months at a time, stir in a little power and influence, and fold it all into a town that has more overused escorts than a Budget Rent-A-Car lot. Add to that thousands of wide-eyed young acolytes flooding into the Below-the-Beltway each year, giving off a heady pheromone brew of ambition and naiveté that an aging political billy goat can smell a mile away. Christ, Washington is like Club Med for doughy, old, unattractive white guys. And don't think I'm exaggerating about how it works down there, folks. Let's put it this way: Newt Gingrich was getting laid. 'Nuff said.

Henry Kissinger once said: "Power is the ultimate aphrodisiac." He was right—no one got more primo skirt during the '70s than Hank Kissinger, and he looked like a troll doll hanging from the rearview mirror of a Volkswagen Beetle.

What trips up politicians is never the actual sex. We know they have sex. We expect them to have sex. What we hate is the arrogance that accompanies the inevitable exposure of the sex as unfailingly as seagulls trailing chum. Somehow, Mr. Smith-Comes-on-to-Washington assumes the American public is as gullible as the twenty-year-old kid he's been bending over his desk on alternate Wednesday evenings for the last two years. He's so full of priapic swagger that when the rumors of hanky-panky start percolating, he just runs his hand through his blow-dried Bobby Goldsboro helmet-cut coif, maybe sprays a shot of Binaca in his mouth, shoots his cuffs, and goes in front of the news cameras and denies everything. Practically insists that Wolf Blitzer hook his nuts up to a polygraph. And he just keeps on smiling that fuck-you-you-can't-touch-me-I'm-bulletproof-because-I-got-my-constituents-a-plow-museum-built-last-year

EVERYBODY'S GUILTY . . . EXCEPT O.J.

One thing I bet Bill Clinton's book won't say is, "I was wrong. I'm sorry." For eight years, he felt everything . . . except for guilt. But why should he? In our therapeutic society, "guilt" has become a dirty word.

Now, I don't want to get off on a rant here, but guilt is simply God's way of letting you know that you're having too good a time.

In the elaborate wardrobe of human emotions, guilt is the itchy wool turtleneck that's three sizes too small. Guilt may be difficult to articulate, but when it surfaces, it's as unwelcome and distinct as Jethro Bodine in the lobby of an Ian Schrager hotel.

What is guilt? Guilt is the pledge drive constantly hammering in our heads that keeps us from fully enjoying the show. Guilt is the reason they put the articles in *Playboy*.

What is the sound of one hand clapping?

Some experience guilt as the voice of their better natures, while for others, it's the voice of an authority figure, like a parent or a teacher. For me, the voice of guilt, interestingly enough, is Jimmie Walker with a slight head cold.

You know, contributing to our recurrent feelings of guilt is the fact that, in our day-to-day lives, we consistently overcommit ourselves, so there is always something we're failing to do. The average American's Day Planner has fewer holes in it than Ray Charles's dartboard. It's gotten to the point where I don't even have time to feel guilty, unless I multitask by also using that time to feel vaguely lackadaisical and kind of twitchy.

It's harder to hide guilt than it is to hide an order of bananas flambé from Al Roker when he's wearing infrared goggles. And I think the reason is that people secretly want to be caught, chastised, and punished, in order to subconsciously prove to themselves that there is indeed an order to the universe that transcends their flawed, limited selves—or, at least, so you can pull down a cool million spouting that line of bullshit in the book you're plugging on *Oprah*.

There are many different types of guilt: healthy guilt, unhealthy guilt, Catholic guilt, and, of course, the newest entry, Condit guilt . . . Representative Gary Condit is a good example of a person who should be wracked with guilt about impeding the investigation of a missing woman. But he is somehow able to speed by the photographers with a smile so big, you would think he was attending his movie premiere at Mann's Chinese Theater. Hey, Gary, make sure to keep that smile on down there when Mephistopheles is rammin' that pitchfork handle up your ass for the rest of eternity.

Ironically, guilt is most likely to visit the people who deserve it the least. Trust me, the only thing that keeps Slobodan Milosevic awake at night is puzzlement over why nobody's nominating him for sainthood, but I can't look at my dog, Mr. Tingles, without cringing at the time two years ago when I accidentally stepped on his tail just as he was leaping at a ball, and he screamed like a Backstreet Boy taking a polo mallet to the nuts. (They have nuts, don't they? It's not like that choir, is it?)

There are some people so predisposed to guilt, when they're born the first thing that comes out of their mouth after being slapped by the doctor is "Harder! Harder!"

I still feel pangs of remorse over an insidious habit I've had since I was a teenager. About three times a week, I like to attend estate auctions and make insulting, lowball bids for prized heirlooms until I'm asked to leave. Take me to the shower, I'm a baaaaaad man.

Many people feel guilty about masturbating. I celebrate it. I say, "Harder! Harder!" What's there to feel guilty about? It's a natural way to relieve stress. Okay, maybe not when someone cuts in front of you in line at the supermarket, but certainly when you get back out to your car.

I've actually written a book about guilt, entitled *Fuck You, I'm Sorry.*

For a long time, I felt tremendously guilty about things that were not in any way my fault, but with the help of an excellent therapist, I have finally accepted that there are things beyond my control. Now I simply breathe deep, release them into the cosmos, and move on. Poverty in distant lands, injustices that were committed long before I was born, that brand-new Mercedes that I rammed repeatedly while trying to wedge my massive, gas-guzzling SUV into a handicapped parking space—Dennis just can't be held responsible for the entire world.

Invented by religion, enforced by the state, and cashed in on by the psychiatric community, guilt is what keeps society from completely unraveling. Yet our culture is rife with politically correct apologists telling us to let go of the shame that binds us, and to treat our mistakes as learning experiences that we have to "heal" from and "put behind us" as quickly as we can. That's just bullshit. If you do something wrong, you *should* feel guilty about it. Guilt is the pruning shears that society developed to prevent you from growing into an even bigger asshole than you already are. I'm sorry I said that.

Of course, that's just my opinion. I could be wrong.